ALSO BY
SEAN PATRICK HANNIFIN

MAKER OF THE TWENTY-FIRST MOON

SON of a DARK
WiZARD

THE DARK WIZARD CHRONICLES
— BOOK ONE —

SON of a DARK

WIZARD

SEAN PATRICK HANNIFIN

MORROWGRAND BOOKS

A Morrowgrand Book
www.morrowgrand.com

ISBN-10: 0692360018
ISBN-13: 978-0692360019

ACKNOWLEDGMENTS

I want to offer a big thank you to my Mom and Dad. Their unending support was essential for having the time and the motivation to work on what many others might consider a frivolous endeavor.

Also, a huge thank you to my friend Scott Pelath, who read my first drafts of each chapter and offered pages and pages of thoughtful notes and insights into what was working and what wasn't. First readers with such attention to detail who are so willing to donate their time are not easy to come by. I feel very fortunate to have had Scott's help with this, and the book is better for it.

ONE

THE FIRST THING Mordock noticed that night was the owl, the way its silhouette careened through the streaks of cold gray rain. He'd never seen an owl so big, and it was odd to find one roaming the north.

The second thing the old man noticed was the river raging below, the way it shook the narrow wooden bridge beneath his feet as it swallowed the muck and garbage spilling in from the dark city's cobblestone streets. He'd never heard water roar so loudly.

The third thing Mordock noticed was the fire, flecks of light on a distant mountain, flickering like a candle's flame. The high towers of the Wizard King's castle were burning.

A hand clutched the old man's shoulder. "Mordock?"

Mordock turned to face the one he'd been waiting for. Oakren was tall, bald, and sported a thin gray beard. He nodded and held out a long staff. It was made of a thick twisted length of black iron. At its top, strands of iron curled in wide spirals like branches of a dead tree, forming the bars of a spherical cage. There was no light inside.

So it was true. The most powerful wizard who had ever lived was gone. Vonlock was dead.

Mordock had thought he would be happy to learn the news. Long had he dreamed of taking Vonlock's position as Head of the Nyrish Council. He took the lightless staff from Oakren, clutching it so tightly that his fingers went white. If someone had the power to kill Vonlock . . .

"Who did this?" Mordock asked.

Oakren's voice quivered. "We must hold council."

T HE CLOCKS were chiming the hour of two in the morning by the time the wizards of the Council of the Nyrish Moon had gathered. They were the eight most powerful wizards from across the twelve kingdoms, some young, most old, some kings, some dreaming of becoming kings. They sat along the sides of a long black marble table with drinks in silver chalices before them. The chair at the head of the table was vacant now. Vonlock's lightless staff sat perched at its side.

Mordock spoke first.

"As I'm certain you've heard by now, Vonlock was killed tonight. Oakren snuck into his castle as soon as we heard rumor of an attack. He brought back Vonlock's staff and—"

"And I insisted for an immediate call to council," Oakren said, rising to his feet. His face was bulky like stone, complementing his gravelly voice. "The one who killed Vonlock has the power to kill us all. He can rid the world of the Nyrish power forever." Oakren leaned forward, pressing his hands on the table. He spoke slowly. "I fear it may be time for us to disband. At least for a decade or so."

Some of the wizards scoffed.

"How'd he do it?" one of them asked. "How'd he kill Vonlock?"

"I don't know," Oakren said.

"Then how can you say—"

"It's *who* killed him that worries me," Oakren said.

"And who is that?"

"I don't know his name," Oakren said. "But I think all the twelve kingdoms will know his name soon enough."

"Why?" a young wizard at the far end of the table asked.

"Have you heard of the Candlewood Prophecy?" Oakren asked, sipping wine from his chalice.

The young wizard chuckled. "Prophecy nonsense?"

Oakren slammed his chalice on the table. "Have you heard of it?"

The young wizard slowly shook his head.

"It was before his time," Mordock said. He spoke gently, as if trying to calm everyone. "But why do you think this is the fulfillment of some old prophecy?"

"Because," Oakren said, turning to Mordock, "the one who killed Vonlock was a *boy*. Eleven years old, twelve at the most. He was commanding a group of Zolen soldiers like a king."

"What does it matter?" one the old wizards said. "It doesn't necessarily mean—"

"You can't just hire Zolen soldiers. They're not mercenaries. They would not follow a *boy* into the castle of the most powerful Wizard King who has ever lived unless they believed in him. Unless they believed in a *prophecy*. Unless they believed he was *chosen*."

"Are you saying," Mordock said, once again speaking gently, "that Vonlock was killed by . . . the *Chosen One*?"

Oakren nodded at the lightless staff beside the empty chair. "No one else could have defeated Vonlock."

"This is absurd!" the young wizard at the end of the table said. "Do you really expect us to believe—"

"I don't care what you believe!" Oakren shouted. "I know what I saw and I know Vonlock is dead! Prophecy or no prophecy, I will not—"

"Wait!" An old wizard waved his hands about. "Wait, wait, wait! The Candlewood Prophecy concerns only the Candlewood family of wizards. Even *if* the prophecy is true, even *if* the boy who killed Vonlock is the Chosen One, even *if* the prophecy has just been fulfilled, why should *we* worry about it? We're not of the Candlewood family. Only Vonlock was."

"So," Oakren said, "if you found the Chosen One at the gates of your castle, would you invite him in for tea?"

"What?"

"He's the *Chosen One!*" Oakren growled. "Who here would not fear to stand before the Chosen One, regardless of the details of his prophecy?"

There was silence.

Oakren nodded. "Therefore I say we should disband."

"If this boy is truly a threat," a wizard with a big bushy mustache said, "disbanding would only make us weaker."

Mordock nodded. "We're stronger as a council."

"We're leaderless," Oakren said. "We're weak. We have never before managed without Vonlock."

"Well," Mordock said, standing from his seat and inching toward Vonlock's vacant chair, "in that case, temporarily, perhaps I could . . ."

"Don't you dare," Oakren said.

"This is no time to fight for Head of Council!" an old wizard said.

"Exactly," Mordock said, "so just temporarily . . ." He took another small step toward the head of the table.

Oakren formed a small orb of blue fire above the palm of his hand. "I am not playing games with you, Mordock."

"Trial!" the young wizard at the end of the table said. "I call for a trial to decide the next Head of Council."

The wizard with the big bushy mustache rushed to a desk along the side of the room and took some paper, some ink, and a quill pen. "I will write a contract to be bound by the Nyrish power."

"Wait!" an old wizard said. "The Chosen One just *killed* the most powerful wizard in the world, and we're preparing a trial of succession?"

"It's trial or disband," Oakren said.

"We *cannot* disband," the bushy-mustached wizard said, dipping his pen in ink and scribbling onto a blank scroll.

"Who wishes to compete?" the young wizard said. "Put a hand on the table." He put his own hand forward.

Mordock grimaced, but put his hand on the table.

Oakren smiled, sliding a hand onto the table as well. "Is this it?" he asked, looking around. "Only three?"

"Come sign your names," the bushy-mustached wizard said. He pinched his fingers together. "And a drop to make it binding."

The three wizards signed their names and left a dab of their own blood on the contract.

"Now then," Mordock said, "to decide tasks . . . I propose we—"

Crash!

Mordock jumped backward as a large raven flew through the room and landed on the back of Vonlock's empty chair.

"Is that a bird?"

"A raven?"

"Where'd it come from?"

"Crashed through the window."

"Impossible."

"Flew right through the glass."

"It's true. Look."

"Look! The staff!"

"It's not lightless anymore!"

"Vonlock is alive?!"

"No, look! The flame is green!"

"Impossible."

"That makes no sense."

"Look! Something on the bird's leg!"

"A note?"

"Who's bird is this?"

"What's going on?"

"Look at the note!"

"Take it!"

"Read it!"

"All right, all right," Oakren said, carefully sliding the tiny scroll from the string tied around the raven's leg. "Let me see." He took a small monocle from his pocket and pushed it over his eye, then unrolled the scroll. He brought it close to his face, squinting and murmuring to himself. Then, after a short silence, he looked up, eyes wide. "He's been listening. He wishes to compete."

"Who?"

"Who?"

"Who?"

Oakren gestured to the staff, a green flame now glowing within its spherical cage. "Vonlock's heir."

"You mean . . ." Mordock said.

Oakren nodded.

The bushy-mustached wizard looked confused. "So *he* survived? How?"

"I don't know," Oakren said, "but council law says Vonlock's heir is automatically a member of the council."

"But . . . But . . ." Mordock said. "He can't be older than thirteen . . ."

"Doesn't matter," Oakren said. "As a member of the council, he must be allowed to compete."

"It's true," the bushy-mustached wizard nodded.

"This is ridiculous," Mordock said.

"I'm sorry," the young wizard said, "but *who* are we talking about?"

"His heir," Oakren said. "Vonlock's heir."

"Vonlock's heir?" the young wizard repeated. "Who's Vonlock's heir?"

An old wizard put his face in his hands. "We should have disbanded."

"It's too late for that," Oakren said.

"Have you ever met the boy?" Mordock asked.

"I know, he's a bit . . ."

"I'm sure he's still listening," the bushy-mustached wizard said.

"Anyway, we signed already," Oakren said. "We are bound by blood to compete."

"I think we just dug our own graves," the bushy-mustached wizard said.

The room sat in silence. The only sound was the night winds whistling through the broken window.

"Maybe not," Mordock said quietly, a thin smile creeping across his lips. "We still haven't set the tasks."

Oakren squinted at him, sliding his monocle back into his pocket. "What are you proposing?" he whispered.

"We'll give him an impossible task."

"Ah," Oakren's eyes went wide. He gestured at Vonlock's empty chair. "Pit him against . . . ?"

Mordock grinned. "We'll send him straight to his own grave."

The young wizard at the end of the table stood up, kicking his chair backward. "No one has answered me!"

All seven other wizards around the table stared at the young man.

"*Who* is Vonlock's heir?" he asked.

"His name is Sorren," Oakren said. "He's Vonlock's son."

TWO

A TALL OLD MAN with long scraggly dark green hair leaned on his iron staff, waiting in front of a large wooden door built into the cavern's wall. A twelve year old walked up beside him, holding the tray of breakfast food he'd been ordered to bring.

The boy's name was Thale. He'd been old Kovola's apprentice for as long as he could remember, learning to make things for wizards, things that only worked with the power of the Nyrish moon. Toves, as they were called. And if you could not be a wizard, being a tovemaster was the next best thing. Of course, he could only make simple things, like clocks and music boxes that didn't need to be wound. But someday he'd learn the secrets of making staffs and portal doors and dark mirrors. Someday.

"Is he awake yet?" Thale asked, inching toward the door.

"Yes, he's been waiting," Kovola said. "Just remember, do not say anything about—"

"About his arm. I know." Kovola had only warned him twenty times. Thale wasn't even sure how Sorren had lost the arm. Kovola had mentioned something about finding him buried in a pile of stones, but nothing more.

Kovola opened the door slowly. "Sorren? We have your breakfast."

Thale followed the old man through the door and into the wide cavern room. Everything was so dark within these cavern walls. Thale wondered if he'd ever see Vonlock's castle again. It didn't seem likely now that the Chosen One and a small army of Zolen soldiers had taken it over.

Still, Thale didn't mind the darkness. He could see in the darkness very well thanks to his tovocular eye. When he was five years old, he'd been attacked by a wandering mountain wolf, and his left eye had been torn from its socket. Rather than giving him a glass eye or an eye patch, Kovola had immediately set about creating a tovocular eye to be placed in the empty eye socket. It looked like a very small spyglass, gold with a dark bluish green lens, and could be removed at night when Thale went to sleep. But when it was in, Thale could see with it, and it worked better than a human eye. Everything was in focus, colors were vibrant, he could zoom in and out on things, and he could see in the dark.

Sorren's room was cold and barren. A large bed sat against the far wall, its blankets crumpled. A table sat close by, piled with metalwork tools and small bits of scrap metal, copper and silver and brass.

Sorren stood by a mirror next to the table, pulling on his long black duster coat, collar up as usual. His hair was a thick mess of black and, as he turned around, Thale saw a pair of thin dark green goggles on his forehead. Sorren was one of the rare wizards whose powers often produced flames and sparks too bright for his own eyes. His skin was pale, almost ghostly white, the reward of a childhood spent in shadows. Like most wizards of the Nyrish power, he was nocturnal, and woke only after sunset.

"Ah, breakfast," Sorren said, eyeing the tray of warm cinnamon bread, fruit, and truddleberry juice.

"Your arms . . ." Thale said.

Kovola nudged him with his staff.

Sorren reached out with his left arm, curling his gloved fingers. It moved with a faint whirring noise.

"You'd never know, would you?" Sorren said, smiling. He pulled the glove off and pushed his sleeve up, revealing his new mechanical arm, an intricate system of brass and silver that moved as naturally as the real thing.

"Hardly the thing you should be doing with your spare time," Kovola said, clearing a space on the table. "You need rest. Thale, tray here."

Sorren slid the glove back on. Kovola may not have cared, but Sorren was not about to waste time resting. He sat at the table, took a sip of juice, and whistled. His raven, Quove, flew to his side and began pecking at the bread.

"Oh," Sorren said, "I'm going to create a portal soon. For Mordock."

"Do you think that wise?" Kovola asked. "You should keep

this place a secret. If the Chosen One knows you are still alive . . ."

"We don't have to worry about Mordock," Sorren said. "And he has my father's staff. I want it back."

"I understand that, but . . ." Kovola seemed hesitant to say something. The old man turned to Thale. "Could you leave us for a moment?"

Thale nodded. Sorren watched as the one-eyed boy left the room, closing the door behind him, then turned to Kovola. "What is it?"

"It's what we've both been avoiding," Kovola said. "We need to decide where best to go into exile and find—"

"Exile?" Sorren interrupted, munching on fruit. "I'm not going into exile."

"Sorren," Kovola said, with that gravely serious voice of his, "your father was assassinated. *Your* assassination was attempted. Eventually they'll realize you survived. You cannot stay in Morrowgrand."

"I'm going to become the next Head of the Nyrish Council," Sorren said, sipping his drink. "I can't do that while in exile."

Kovola sighed and shook his head. "You're thirteen years old, Sorren. The Nyrish Council is full of Wizard Kings and old powerful sorcerers. A thirteen year old Head of Council? It's impractical. It's impossible. You are only going to get yourself killed."

"Have some cinnamon bread," Sorren said, shoving a crumbly piece of bread in the old man's hand and rising to his feet. "I need to find my journals. I haven't made a portal in years."

"Sorren . . ." Kovola started, but said nothing else. Quove flew to Kovola and landed on his wrist, pecking at the bread in his hand until the old man angrily shooed the bird away.

"SORREN," Mordock said, stepping through the portal with an obviously fake smile. "The entire council was so relieved when we heard you had survived."

"Good for them," Sorren said, studying the staff in Mordock's hand. It didn't look to be damaged at all. The green flame burning at the top confirmed that the staff belonged to him now. His father's color had been purple. Sorren held out a hand. "I'll take my staff now."

Mordock seemed to ignore him as the shadows of the portal behind him faded back into a tall mirror's glass. "You must be so broken inside," he said. "I mean, to lose your father and your castle and your claim to Morrowgrand's throne all in one night . . . I can't imagine what you must be going through."

"My staff," Sorren said.

"The council has actually decided to hold a service in memory of your fallen father," Mordock said, "so that his memory may live on."

Sorren whispered the words of a spell in his mind. The staff tore out of Mordock's hand, flew across the room, and Sorren caught it. "Well, have fun with that."

Mordock grimaced and rubbed his palms together as if the force of the spell had stung his skin. Oh well. He'd asked for it. "Come now, Sorren, don't you want to honor the memory of your father?"

Sorren knew neither Mordock nor any other wizard of the Nyrish Council truly honored his father or his memory. Mordock was only trying to pour salt on an open wound. It would not work.

"Did the council decide on the tasks for the trial?" Sorren asked.

Mordock nodded and pulled a small scroll from the inside of his coat. "It's only one task. Whoever achieves it becomes Head of Council."

Sorren turned the staff in his hands, learning the feel of the curves and twists of the cold iron, the warmth of the green flame on the side of his face. It had been passed down through the Candlewood family for centuries and was more solid than stone. He'd always imagined being much older when it would finally become his own.

Sorren held out a hand to take the scroll.

Mordock held it close to himself. "I must warn you," he said, "this is no game. This is how wizards die. We've agreed that since you have not bound yourself to the trial with blood, you may choose to withdraw if you wish."

"How kind of you," Sorren said, repeating the seizing spell in his mind, sending the scroll flying out of Mordock's grip and into his own. He slowly unrolled it until he could see the three small dark red stains of the other wizards' dried blood. He held his staff in his elbow, whispered a spell to prick his ring finger, and smeared his own blood along the bottom of the page.

"Now I am bound," he said.

Mordock did not seem amused by this. "You arrogant fool.

You are going to die like your father and you will not be mourned."

Sorren whispered a spell to reopen the portal behind Mordock. "Goodbye, Mordock. I'm sure you're very busy today."

Mordock glared at Sorren, then turned and walked back through the portal. Sorren waited until the shadows of the portal faded away before unrolling the rest of the scroll. Quove flew to his shoulder as he read over it.

Most of the scroll simply outlined the standard procedures for a trial of succession, and what being bound by blood in the Nyrish power meant. The task set for the trial was written near the bottom. It was only four words.

Defeat the Chosen One.

THREE

THE NAME OF ATLORUS spread through the land of Morrowgrand like the winds of a storm, the young boy who had defeated the tyrannical Wizard King Vonlock. They called Atlorus the savior, Morrowgrand's lost prince, the Chosen One. They told stories about him in the taverns, sang songs about him on street corners. Children in village squares reenacted his triumphant battle against the dark wizard, and at night their parents promised them they'd soon live in a better world. They destroyed the dead king's statues, memorials Vonlock had built in honor of his own power. They toppled his gallows, where he'd sentenced men to hang if they dared even whisper a word against him. They threw his guards in jail, even as they claimed their loyalty was never true.

Yet no one said a word about how Vonlock was defeated, how a boy so young and powerless could kill a wizard so mighty. No one had a clue as to how Atlorus had done it.

Walking the roads at night with Thale, Sorren guessed he

was one of the few who had actually seen the Chosen One's face when they confronted each other that night. Sorren had seen the face flash before him each night since, the wide eyes, the pale skin, the quivering breath, the utter fear. The stories and songs portrayed the Chosen One as some miraculous angelic warrior, a strong and noble child. Sorren knew the truth. Atlorus was a coward.

So how had he done it?

Sorren and Thale kept in the shadows of the sidewalks, away from the murky light of the flickering street lanterns. Sorren also kept the flame of his staff too small to draw attention; it was the size of a speck of dust. It was unlikely that commoners in this part of Morrowgrand would know Sorren's face, but he wanted to be safe. When they came to the tavern, they waited on the other side of the street, under a street lamp near the edge of the forest.

"How well can you see the tavern from here?" Sorren asked.

Thale's tovocular eye gave a faint mechanical *bzzt*. "I can see a fly on a sweaty man's forehead through the window."

"Do you know what Zolen soldiers wear when they're in public?"

"Dark gray coats with three blood-red lines on the sleeve?"

Sorren patted Thale on the shoulder. "Tell me when you see a Zolen soldier leave the tavern. Then you can go back."

"What are you going to do?" Thale asked.

"I want to meet him."

"Does Kovola know we're here?"

"You can tell him when you go back."

"Are you going to . . . You're not going to . . . Are you?"

"I'm going to meet him," Sorren said, "and I'm going to get a few answers."

"Yes, but . . . Are you going to . . ."

Sorren looked at Thale with a blank expression, then suddenly slapped himself on the neck. "Bah," he said, studying the palm of his hand. "Mosquito." He brushed his hands together. "Treacherous little things."

Thale made no more attempts to ask whatever question he was apparently too afraid to ask. Fair enough, Sorren thought, since he knew he didn't know the answer.

IT WAS A QUIET NIGHT for Bringlen. He sat alone at a table near the back of the tavern. His cup was now empty, and his thirst was gone. He leaned back in his chair with his eyes half closed, wandering on the edge of sleep, half-listening to a nearby lute player's song. The tune was traditional but the words were new.

> *Goodbye, Vonlock, now meet the flame!*
> *For all the wicked pay a toll.*
> *Now may the devil write your name!*
> *Now may his fire take your soul!*

Days ago, Bringlen was proud to have been part of the small group of Zolen soldiers who had helped Atlorus break into the dark wizard's castle. As a Zolen soldier, he hardly ever ventured out of the small but peaceful Zolen Republic. Zolen soldiers were proud, well-trained, and mostly kept to themselves, defending the borders of their small independent nation. Sneaking into Morrowgrand to help assassinate its greedy king had been a bizarre and risky mission for them, but they knew if they could earn Morrowgrand's trust, the expansive kingdom would make a powerful ally for their nation. After their victory, Bringlen had imagined journeying home on a new horse, embracing his wife at the door of their home with large bags of reward money and a wonderful new story for their four year old son.

But over the past few nights a shadow had passed over him, a subtle misery. It was made of every song he heard in every tavern, of every story he caught on the street. It was Atlorus who was getting all the glory for Vonlock's defeat. Not that the young boy didn't deserve a good share of it. But what about the Zolen soldiers? Was Bringlen's name to be forgotten completely? Was history to pay no tribute whatsoever to the Zolen soldiers who risked their lives for the Kingdom of Morrowgrand? Where were the songs for the soldiers? Where were the stories? Atlorus could not have done it alone. Yes, he was the one who actually defeated Vonlock, but the Zolen soldiers were the ones who led him through the castle. And what thanks did Bringlen get for it? A small bag of reward money and a pat on the back. That was it. Atlorus would be praised and celebrated for the rest of his life while Bringlen was already forgotten.

Bringlen knew his envy for the young Chosen One was petty and vain. He knew he should've been thankful for the dark wizard's defeat like the rest of Morrowgrand. Still, envy twisted his heart, and so far both ale and whiskey had failed to wash it away. So Bringlen was not yet ready to journey home. He was waiting for the shadows to pass, for the weather to grow warmer, for the songs he heard everywhere to sound like music again.

Bringlen jerked his head up as four men with bottles in their hands surrounded the table.

"Can we sit here, sir?" one of them asked. "Can we join you? There's nowhere else."

Bringlen rose to his feet. "I'm just leaving." No sense hanging around here. It stank and the music was awful.

Leaving the tavern, Bringlen folded his arms, shivering in the night's chill and watching the fog of his breath curl up toward the stars. The moons were bright tonight. There was the blue Nyrish moon, a large blue disk in the black sky, its dark craters and scars clearly visible. Wizards who drew their power from the light of the Nyrish moon were rare, but also the most powerful, and since they often abused their power, they were known as dark wizards. Then there was the Wortax moon with its swirling shades of green, much smaller than the Nyrish. There used to be wizards of the Wortax power, in ancient times. But their powers were weaker and they eventually disappeared.

The shadow man watches, don't walk alone, Bringlen thought. It was some old superstition. When the moons were full and close together, they resembled a wild man's eyes.

Bringlen made his way across the street. The inn he was staying at was just through the forest, on the other side. It would only be a short walk.

As he passed under a street lamp, he noticed a large raven sitting atop it. It seemed to turn its head as he passed underneath, as if it were watching him. Bringlen thought it curious. He'd never seen a raven on a winter's night.

The trees hid the moons as he walked into the forest, their twisted branches still bare, victims of a long winter. It was almost too dark to see anything and Bringlen cursed himself for not leaving the tavern sooner or bringing a lantern. There were lights just barely visible in the distance through the trees, almost like stars. The lamps of the inn.

I just have to follow the light, Bringlen told himself. He kept his steps slow and cautious. He didn't want to trip on some fallen log or catch his foot on some exposed tree root.

Slowly, he moved forward.

Step by step.

He kept his gaze on the lights in the distance.

Something scraped against the bark of a tree on his left. Bringlen froze and jerked his head to the side, but all was darkness.

A wolf, Bringlen thought. *I should've brought my sword.*

He kept still. The night seemed to grow colder, chilling him even under his thick gray coat, as if his body warmth was being drained. Something broke a twig, shuffled through the leaves. The creature was moving closer.

Bringlen patted his coat pockets for the knife he knew he didn't have.

A light appeared. A bright green light. No, it was fire. An orb of fire! It shone through the forest, casting a green glow on the surrounding trees, giving shape to the figure of a young man in a long dark coat.

And then Bringlen recognized the staff. It was Vonlock's staff. That twisted length of iron, those spirals wrapping the green flame. Centuries old, he'd seen it in more than a few historic paintings.

"Vonlock." Bringlen said the name without thinking.

"No," the figure replied, moving forward.

No, of course not. This was a boy. Younger, thinner, shorter. Bringlen squinted, trying to make out the face behind the green flame. "Who are you?"

The boy held out the staff, revealing his face. Bringlen recognized it, but before he could recall the boy's name, tree branches were wrapping themselves around him, grabbing his arms, slithering across his chest and his neck, pulling him backward, lifting him into the air. Bringlen fought against them, kicking and thrashing, but it was no use. The branches were under the control of some dark spell. They held Bringlen as though they meant to crush him. After a moment, he relaxed, caught his breath, and looked down at the boy with the staff.

"You?" Bringlen said. "The son?"

"You don't know my name?" the boy said.

"Sorren?"

"You helped Atlorus kill my father, yes?" Sorren asked.

"You're dead," Bringlen said. "I saw you die. Crushed by stone."

"And my father?"

Bringlen gasped for breath as the branch around his neck tightened. "Your father?"

"How did my father die?"

"Please!" Bringlen cried, squirming in the branches, trying to find some air. "Please! I can't breathe!"

Sorren repeated his question slowly and calmly. "How did my father die?"

"I don't know! I didn't see!"

"You didn't see?"

"Atlorus killed him! He did it alone! Nobody saw!"

"Alone?"

Bringlen took a moment to try to catch his breath. He'd lost feeling in his hands and his right leg. At any moment his bones would begin to crunch. "He went into the throne room alone, wouldn't let anyone else in. Said he had to face the Dark One alone to fulfill the prophecy. Nobody saw! I swear to you, nobody saw!"

"So why did you trust him?" Sorren asked. "How did you know he could defeat my father?"

"I didn't," Bringlen said between gasps. "None of us did. It was a chance, and we took it."

"You must've had some reason to believe in him."

"It was Gashdane," Bringlen said. The world was becoming blurry.

"Gashdane?" Sorren repeated. "Your commander? Head of the Zolen army?"

"He said the boy fit the prophecy. Born in the right place on the right night. He said he'd seen proof."

"Where is Gashdane?"

"He's with the boy," Bringlen said. "He stayed with the boy. They took an airship to fly across Morrowgrand."

"Winter's an odd season to go exploring."

"The kingdom is his reward," Bringlen said, his voice barely above a whisper now. "Who do you think they're going to crown the new king?"

Bringlen watched as Sorren turned his gaze to the forest floor and began pacing. The branches loosened and Bringlen took in a full breath. He head was pounding, but feeling was returning to his hands and leg. He was too weak to struggle. Every muscle ached.

Sorren looked up at him. "You really haven't been much help."

"I've told you all I know."

Sorren shook his head. "But it's not enough."

"Please. Sorren. I have a child. I have a son."

"An odd thing to plea."

"What are you going to do to me?"

Sorren flicked his scepter to the side, and the branches flew out from under Bringlen. Too weak to even flail his arms and try to break his own fall, the soldier came crashing to the ground. He slowly rolled onto his back, panting for breath. His joints stung, and every breath felt like shards of glass.

Sorren's face hovered over his. "Are you going to tell everyone that I'm alive?" the young wizard asked. "You could write some new songs. The ones I've heard aren't very good. And they don't get everything right, do they?"

"I swear I won't tell a soul."

Sorren put the end of his staff on the back of Bringlen's outstretched hand. Bringlen flinched, expecting some spell to blast through his skin, but nothing happened.

"What was Atlorus like?" Sorren asked.

Bringlen stared up into Sorren's eyes, but the young wizard showed no emotion. "He was . . ." Bringlen thought for a moment. "He was quiet. He seemed . . . worn out, weary . . . like he was weighed down. But he . . . he knew he could do it. He knew he'd win the battle."

"The battle hasn't ended," Sorren said. Then the green light of his staff faded and he was gone.

Slivers of blue and green moonlight pierced through the bare forest trees. Bringlen was left on the forest floor gazing skyward, catching his breath, waiting for his strength to return.

FOUR

SORREN SAT in his cavern room. No candles or lanterns were lit, but the glow of his staff gave light to the pages of the journals and books open on the table before him. He had been busy for the past several hours, studying how airships worked and creating a few new tools he'd need soon. His new arm made things easier. It moved with a steady precision his flesh-and-blood arm didn't have.

As he studied the spells of the Nyrish power, he suddenly realized that his father would never give him any more lessons. It hadn't hit him until that moment. His father's lessons were over forever. He tried not to think of it. It made him feel hallow and empty. Incomplete. Almost sick. For a short moment, he wished he hadn't survived.

Someone knocked on the door. "Are you awake?" It was Kovola.

"Come in," Sorren said.

Kovola entered, carrying a small scroll in one hand, his face pale and tired as usual. "Agh," he said, shivering, wrapping his arms under his cloak. "Freezing in here."

"I'm working," Sorren said. Sometimes concentration made him absentmindedly drain his surroundings of energy. At times, it was a useful feature of the Nyrish power. Usually it only annoyed people.

"Your inconduction is far worse than your father's," Kovola said. "You must learn to control it. You'll freeze us all to death." The old man stood before Sorren's table and dropped the small scroll onto the books.

"What is it?" Sorren asked, not putting down the rod he was enchanting with an elementary fire spell.

"Defeat the Chosen One?" Kovola said. "Is that what you're trying to do with all this?" He motioned at the mess of books and tools and scraps of metal spread around the table.

Sorren sat back in his chair and glanced around. "I know I'll need more."

"Are you really as blind as all that?" Kovola asked.

Sorren slid his green goggles down over his eyes. "Watch out." The last part of the enchantment required a spell that would create a blinding flash of light.

Kovola quickly turned his head, shutting his eyes tightly and shielding them with a hand.

For a half-second, the room blazed in a blinding bright shade of gold.

Sorren slid his goggles back to his forehead and held out the rod. He turned it in his hands, giving it one last inspection.

Kovola turned back to face the young wizard. "Don't you realize what they're doing?" he said, picking up the scroll and unrolling it. "No one is actually competing with you. It's a trick. The council is sending you directly to the Chosen One. They're trying to kill you."

"I know."

Kovola stood there as if waiting for a more elaborate response. "You don't care?"

"It's expected," Sorren said, placing the now finished fire rod on the table. "It doesn't change anything."

"So you're going to play their game? You're going to try to defeat the Chosen One?"

Sorren stood up, stretched, and made his way to his bookshelf full of books and journals, lighting lanterns along the wall with a whispered charm as he went. "I *will* defeat the Chosen One," he said, scanning the shelves. "And I need a map."

"Thale said you tortured someone?" Kovola said. "A Zolen soldier?"

"I met a Zolen soldier and asked him some questions." Sorren pulled a book of maps from the shelf. "He wasn't very helpful."

"If you want to try to defeat the Chosen One, I'm not going to stop you," Kovola said. Sorren could feel the old man's icy stare even as he flipped through the book's pages. "But do not drag Thale into your plans."

"He has a good eye."

"He's far behind in his lessons," Kovola said. "At his rate, I'm not sure he'll ever even be a mediocre tove maker."

Sorren turned and met the old man's stare. "I don't force Thale to do anything."

"You seem to be missing my point."

"I'm not going to put him in any danger," Sorren said. And

he meant it. Thale was the closest thing he had to a brother.

Kovola was silent. He just stood there, staring at Sorren as if he couldn't decide whether or not to believe him. Then he held up the scroll and said, "If you continue with this, you're putting all three of us in danger."

Sorren collected a few more books from the shelves and brought them back to the table. He sat down slowly, spent a few moments sorting through his journals and finding a fountain pen, then looked up at Kovola. "Why do you stay with me?"

"I swore an oath of loyalty to the Candlewood family. You're the last one left."

Sorren dipped his pen in ink and began scratching notes on an empty journal page. "I need help getting an airship," he said.

"We don't have the money to buy an airship," Kovola said, "nor the materials to build one."

"That leaves one option."

"Sorren . . ."

"Meet me in the room of mirrors in an hour."

FIVE

NY MIRROR could be enchanted into a portal door as long as it was appropriately flat, reflective, and unbroken. Tall mirrors could be stepped through easily, while smaller hand mirrors could be used for transporting small items, engaging in face-to-face conversations, or spying on anyone with a mirror nearby. A set of two mirrors were needed for two-way portals, but with the proper set of coordinates, and enough skill in portal making, one mirror could serve as a one-way portal to almost anywhere on the planet.

Sorren was enchanting the mirror before him as a one-way portal door that would open on a rocky mountainside in Morrowgrand's southwest. The Ashwood Mountains, as they were called. It was on those mountains that Landoran airships delivered their cargo to Morrowgrand traders, importing goods like textiles, crystals, glowstones, and foreign metals.

"So you want to steal a cargo airship?" Kovola asked, as he and Sorren stood before the mirror. Sorren was pointing his staff toward the mirror, finishing the enchantment.

"It'll be easy," Sorren said. "No one will miss a little cargo ship. Pirates are seizing them all the time." He whispered the final phrases of the portal enchantment in his mind. He then muttered another spell under his breath and the reflections in the mirror faded to darkness. Slowly, the image of the night sky appeared beyond the glass, countless stars surrounding a pair of half moons. The black silhouettes of coniferous trees lined the bottom of the image. The climate was warmer in southwestern Morrowgrand, and the Ashwood Mountains were home to many small patches of forest.

Sorren stepped forward, peering into the image. He had always wanted to explore the Ashwood Mountains. They were the setting of many ancient legends and no traveler claimed to know all their secrets. And the sky seemed so much bigger on the mountainsides. Vonlock had once promised him they'd one day walk the mountains together, but it had never happened. Sorren gripped the staff tightly in his flesh-and-blood hand.

"Ready?" Kovola asked.

Sorren didn't answer immediately. He was too busy taking in the sight of the wide skies and the countless stars.

Then he gathered the supplies he had set by the mirror. The fire rod he had prepared earlier, which would melt through locks. A Nyrish lucator, a fist-sized instrument made of copper and shaped like an egg. When installed on an airship's engine, it would allow the ship to be powered by the Nyrish power rather than regular fuel. Finally, a small mirror in a simple black wooden frame, just big enough for Sorren and Kovola to crawl through. It would serve as a return portal as soon as Sorren enchanted it. Without it, it would be a long journey back to these northern caverns, even in an airship.

"Here," Sorren said, handing Kovola the small mirror. "Don't break it."

Kovola took it without a word.

"Where are you going?"

Sorren turned to see Thale standing in the back of the room, the lens of his tovocular eye twisting in and out.

"Tend to your lessons," Kovola said sharply, clearly annoyed.

"I finished all the readings you assigned," Thale said.

"Read them again."

"We're stepping to the other end of Morrowgrand," Sorren said. "To the Ashwood Mountains."

"Is the Chosen One there?" Thale asked.

"Back to your lessons!" Kovola said.

"I'm only commandeering an airship," Sorren said. He gave a quick whistle, and Quove flew out of the shadows behind Thale to stand on Sorren's right shoulder. "But there *is* something you can do for me."

"Sorren . . ." Kovola said.

"Find my pocket watch beside my bed," Sorren said, "return here, and time how long this takes me."

And with that, Sorren turned to the mirror and stepped through its glass.

"And while you watch time tick away," Kovola said, "*study.*"

"I will," Thale said very reassuringly.

Kovola sighed and followed Sorren through the mirror.

HOFF WAS SICK of flying airships. The long hours adjusting directions and speeds over wild ocean weather. The cramped-up stuffiness of the small navigation room. The smell of old food, dirty laundry, and the sweat of other men. It was always too hot or too cold.

At least Vonlock was gone. News of his death had spread quickly through the skies as passing airships eagerly shared the stories they'd heard. Perhaps under the rule of a new king, Hoff would see more business in Morrowgrand, and flying there would actually be worth the journey.

Hands on the airship's helm, Hoff caught sight of his destination. A row of twelve tall torches along the Ashwood Mountains in the distance were a welcome sight after more than a week spent over ocean waters. The sight always gave Hoff a sigh of relief.

It took half an hour to guide the small cargo airship down and around the mountain peaks. He brought his ship to a fixed-float beside a rocky mountain clearing not far from the torches, opened the airship's cargo hatch, and lowered the loading bridge.

Leaving the confines of the navigation room, Hoff pounded on the doors that lined the hallway outside. "Wake up, you worthless sacks of dirt!" he shouted, his voice coarse and gurgly from years of glowstone smoking. "Wake up! Time to unload." As his three loaders stumbled out of their rooms rubbing their eyes and looking indifferent, Hoff continued shouting at them, his orders colored with words only sailors of the sky could appreciate.

Stepping down the loading bridge and onto the rocky mountainside, Hoff took in a deep breath of the warm mountain air, filled with its smells of dirt and mountain stone and ocean winds.

A small hut sat across the mountain clearing, its windows lit, thick gray smoke puffing from its chimney. A small bald man was already emerging from it, his arms in his coat pockets, trudging his way toward Hoff. Hoff recognized him, even at such a distance. It was Nottlod. He'd been managing this mountainside's imports for as long as Hoff could remember. He grinned as he drew near, and Hoff shook his hand.

"Hoff," Nottlod said, his voice as soft as a child's. "On time as usual. How was your flight?"

"Too cramped and stuffy as always."

"Good, good," Nottlod said. "More carpets and tapestries, yes?" Hoff's men were already beginning to unload the ship, setting large wooden crates in rows nearby.

"They seem to sell well enough," Hoff said.

"Nobody weaves tapestries in Morrowgrand," Nottlod said, pulling a small piece of parchment and a fountain pen from his pocket. "Sign here."

Hoff took the parchment and looked it over, making sure the numbers added up and the price was right. "Nottlod, tell me. Are the stories true?"

"The stories?"

Hoff signed the parchment and handed it back to Nottlod

with the pen. "Is Vonlock dead?"

Nottlod raised his eyebrows and nodded, a look of bliss on his face. "Gone forevermore. Killed by a boy named Atlorus, I've heard. It was all foretold by some old prophecy." Nottlod looked up at the sky, as if suddenly entranced by the stars. "Makes you wonder, doesn't it?"

Hoff had no idea what the little man was talking about.

"If a child could kill Vonlock . . ." Nottlod went on, "if some wild prophecy like that could come true . . . What else can the stars see? What sort of stories are they telling now?"

"Have you actually seen him?" Hoff asked. "This child . . . This Atlos?"

"*Atlorus*," Nottlod said, turning his gaze from the heavens and pulling a bag of coins from another pocket. He handed the payment over to Hoff. "No, of course I haven't actually seen him. Why? Do you think it's all a lie?"

Hoff shrugged, untying the bag and emptying a small portion of the coins onto his palm. "It only sounds like a child's storybook to me." His hid the coins in a pocket inside his jacket and retied the bag, sliding it into another pocket. "But as long as Vonlock's dead, I don't really care about anything else."

"Maybe I'll travel north to the castle," Nottlod said, "and see if I can catch a glimpse of the boy myself. I've never had any excitement like that before. You know what they call him? What they call the boy who defeated Vonlock?"

"The . . . the . . . great and powerful boy?"

"The Chosen One."

Hoff laughed. It came out of him like a storm, a strong

gurgly laugh that made his stomach hurt.

"Why is that funny?" Nottlod asked, looking a little insulted.

"You Morrowgrands," Hoff said. "You've been living in the shadow of this dark wizard for so long, you're romanticizing his death. Prophecies and Chosen Ones."

Hoff laughed again, but Nottlod said nothing. Hoff tried to stop, but Nottlod was walking away before Hoff could relax.

The Chosen One, Hoff repeated in his mind. *Poor Morrowgrands, the simpleminded fools.*

For the next fifteen minutes, Hoff watched his men unload the ship, barking at them every now and then to go faster. He eventually grew tired, sat on one of the crates, took a pipe and a couple glowstone marbles from his pocket, and began smoking between gagging coughs. His eyes were transfixed on the craters of the Nyrish moon almost directly above when one of his men approached.

"Captain," he said, "look. Over there. Something happened to Nottlod."

"Hmm?" Hoff lowered his pipe and peered over his shoulder. In the distance, Nottlod's body was lying face down on the ground in front of his small hut.

"Keep unloading," Hoff said as he slid off the crate. He couldn't run with his terrible lungs, but he walked as fast as he could toward the fallen man.

"Nottlod?" Hoff called out. "You all right? Nottlod?"

When he reached the little man's side, he coughed and tried to catch his breath. Nottlod wasn't moving. Hoff knelt down and grabbed Nottlod's shoulder, turning the man over onto his back. He put two fingers on the Nottlod's neck, checking for a pulse. The man's skin was warm and he was still breathing.

"Nottlod?" Hoff said, keeping his gurgly voice as low and calm as possible. "Nottlod?" He shook the man's shoulder.

Nottlod groaned. Good, he was alive. He must've just fallen down or something.

Hoff scooped the small man in his arms and carried him into his hut. The small room beyond the front door was bathed in the warm glow of firelight. A desk sat near the window, piled with papers and log books. Before a wide fireplace sat a large cushioned chair with a blanket tossed over its arm.

Hoff gently set Nottlod in the chair and pulled the blanket over him. The little man let out another groan as if he were lost in a dream, and his eyes fluttered open. "What?" he said, his voice weak. "Hoff? Why are you here? What happened?"

Hoff studied Nottlod's eyes. Hoff wasn't an expert, but the little man seemed to be healthy, only exhausted. "You must've collapsed outside. Exhaustion I suppose."

"Exhaustion?" Nottlod repeated.

"Just get some rest," Hoff said. "We're almost finished unloading, then we'll be on our way."

"Yes," Nottlod said, nestling his head into the chair's back cushion. "Yes, so exhausted."

Hoff peered around the room, considering stealing something. Now would be the perfect opportunity. But the thought vanished from his mind when he noticed something strange.

Hoff made his way to the front door. The silver door knob and the lock under it were completely misshapen. They looked to be oozing down the door, as if they'd somehow melted. Hoff cautiously put a finger on the drooping metal. It was cool to the touch.

Just outside the door, something moved, some black flag twisted in the air. Hoff gasped and took a step back before realizing it was only some stupid bird fluttering about. Hoff watched as it flew around in small spirals before landing on the rocky ground in front of him. A large raven, it looked like. Hoff thought it very strange. He'd never seen a raven on these mountainsides. For a moment, Hoff could've sworn the raven was looking at him, studying him.

"Bah!" Hoff shouted, raising his arms and racing toward the bird. It quickly flew away and Hoff stood there and laughed and coughed until his throat stung.

He froze when he looked back toward his airship. All three of his men were lying across the boxes, their arms and legs sprawled out, dangling down from the crates.

"Hey!" Hoff called out, walking toward them and waving his arms. "Hey, you putrid filth rags, what are you doing?" The less polite words he called out as he neared them did just as little to wake them.

When he stood beside one of his lazy loaders, he raised a hand and slapped the man hard across the face. The man's eyes went wide and he sat up.

Hoff grunted. "You made me hurt my hand, you rat scum! What do you think you're doing? I don't pay you to nap!"

The man put a hand on the side of his neck. "Something touched me."

"What are you talking about?"

The man looked at his boss, his face pale, as if he'd just seen someone die. "Something touched my neck. Cold as ice. It drained me. I could feel it draining me."

"Draining you?"

"Like it was stealing my energy." He looked at Hoff with watery eyes. "Oh, captain! It's a spirit! The spirit of the mountain! The woman who wanders, looking for her lost child! I've been touched by the wandering woman! I've been touched by a spirit! I've been cursed! I've been—"

Hoff slapped him again with his other hand. "Enough of your madness, you mindless wad of wolf carcass! Get back to work!"

The man trembled, tears dripping from his eyes, and he pointed to something behind Hoff.

Hoff turned around. For a brief second, he thought he saw a shadow pass in front of an airship window. A chill ran up his spine, and goosebumps rose along his arms.

"Spirit," the man whispered.

"Shut your face," Hoff grunted, watching the windows. "It must be pirates."

"But captain, I felt—"

"I said shut your face."

Hoff had often wondered what he would do if he were ever threatened by pirates. Would he put his hands up and surrender like a frightened child, letting the pirates take whatever they wanted? Or would he give the pirates the fight they deserved? "And I got this scar killing pirates," was something Hoff had always dreamed of saying with honesty. Perhaps he'd earn that scar tonight.

"When a pirate steps onto my ship," Hoff said, "he steps onto his grave. Or into his graveyard. Or something." Hoff regretted that he had not daydreamed this moment nearly enough. He turned to the man beside him and put a hand on his shoulder. "If I don't make it tonight, let my name live on in your stories." Not waiting for a reply, he turned to his ship and walked toward the loading bridge.

Hoff kept a sword in the navigation room, hidden behind a loose board on the back wall. Weaponry had been forbidden on cargo ships by order of Vonlock, but Hoff knew he'd need one someday. He wasn't about to lose his ship without a fight.

Climbing up the loading bridge, Hoff realized all the lanterns had been extinguished. Fortunately, he knew his ship well. He knew every turn, every doorway, how many footsteps it took to walk every hall. He knew where the floor creaked and sloped. He knew how to make no sound.

He inched his way through the airship's narrow passages, down halls and up staircases. At last, he came to the navigation room, moonlight pouring through its windows. The sky outside was cloudless, full of its countless stars, while black shadows of distant mountains ran along the edge of the horizon, as if some large portrait of the night sky had been torn in half.

Hoff kept in the shadows, listening for signs that someone else was on the ship, but he heard nothing. Still, he knew he wasn't alone. He could feel it in the stillness of things. The darkness was alive. It was breathing and waiting and watching.

The air was cold. Too cold for this part of Morrowgrand. The tips of Hoff's fingers and the edges of his ears were going numb. Maybe he had only smoked too many glowstones tonight. How could it be so freezing?

Satisfied that the navigation room was as empty as it appeared, Hoff stepped into the moonlight and, with his hands sliding across the wall, made his way to his hidden sword.

Toosh!

Hoff jumped as something crashed against one of the windows. Hoff spun around to see the raven just beyond the glass, its wings flapping wildly, its head drilling into the window as if it expected it could just fly through. *Toosh!* It slammed its whole body into the glass. *Toosh! Toosh!* Again and again, as if possessed by some demon, the raven smacked its head into the glass so forcefully that Hoff expected the glass to crack or explode into a thousand shards.

But nothing happened and the raven flew away.

Hoff took a deep breath and turned back to his work, pulling a board from the wall and sliding a hand into the narrow gap. He grabbed the sword within and pulled it out. It sang a high tone as Hoff accidentally tapped its end against the wall, but it was music to Hoff, like the voice of an angel. The sword was long and narrow, perfect for stabbing a man between his ribs and through his heart. Hoff knew exactly how to do it too. He'd worked with swords in his youth, reducing countless straw men to mere piles of straw.

He held the sword at his side and glanced into the darkness beyond the navigation room door. "All right," he said. "I know you're there."

No answer.

"Come now," Hoff called out, "don't be a coward. There is a place in the netherworld for you, and I will open its door."

Still nothing.

How does one tempt the darkness? Hoff thought. Sword in hand, he turned to the airship controls behind him and pulled a lever, turned a cog, and spun the helm. The airship shook and groaned, waking from its rest, and began to move, floating, turning slowly to the side and rising from the mountain.

"Now you cannot escape," Hoff said.

And a response came from the darkness, a whisper, like a winter wind through a forest. Hoff turned toward the shadows, facing the icy breeze. His arms trembled and he saw his breath on the air. He realized his guest was no sky pirate or mountain spirit.

"Who are you?" Hoff called out, clutching his sword tightly. "What do you want?"

"The ship is mine now," came a whisper from the dark.

"You cannot have it," Hoff said, pointing his sword at the shadows.

A dark form stepped forward into the moonlight. A silhouette, like a moving shadow. The moonlight seemed to have no effect on it. It was shorter than Hoff, its body narrow. It looked as if it were dressed in a long coat, carrying a long staff in one hand. It took slow steps forward, reaching out an arm as if it meant to take the sword.

There was still an icy breeze in the air, and it seemed to whisper a thousand different things, like a thousand children chanting in the far distance.

"You cannot take my ship," Hoff said. His voice quivered and he held his sword close. "You cannot take my ship." It had become a plea.

The shadow figure continued forward, its hand out-stretched. No, it wasn't going for the sword, Hoff realized. It was reaching for his throat.

Hoff knew there would be death in that touch. "Get back," he warned.

"The ship is mine now," the figure repeated, its voice no longer a whisper. It was a male voice, sounded young.

Hoff raised his sword and swung it at the figure's out-stretched arm. He felt it strike flesh, and the shadow figure recoiled, stumbling to the side.

Hoff raised his sword again, preparing to strike another blow.

But the sword was pulled from his clutch as if it had a will of its own. It lashed through the air, glinting in the moonlight, then became a shadow, part of the figure's silhouette. The figure swung it to the side and it flew through the air and through a side window, exploding through the glass.

In that moment, Hoff thought he saw the darkness in his own soul, all his ugly pride and dishonesty and greed alive and writhing like demons in some other world, waiting for him to come, and he knew he was not prepared to die. He collapsed to his knees and tried to beg, but could not find the words. He tried to shout, but could not find his voice.

And then the young shadow figure dropped his staff and lunged forward, catching Hoff's face in his hands, so cold they seemed to burn. Hoff looked into the shadow figure's eyes, bluish green, a young pale face. Then he felt his strength fade away as the world turned to darkness.

"The ship is mine now."

*   *   *   *   *

"**H**OFF?" a voice called out. "Hoff?"

Hoff opened his eyes to the sight of the Nyrish moon. The air was warm. He was lying on rocky mountain ground. There were no signs of the demons he thought he had seen. He sat up, his arms weak.

"Hoff?"

Hoff turned to see his three men running toward him down the mountainside, large torches in their hands.

"Hoff!" one of them called out. "Hoff! There you are!"

Hoff stood up as the men approached. "What happened?" he asked.

"We've been looking for you for hours," one of his men said. "You flew away without us, and Raskin said something about pirates . . ."

"Spirits," Raskin said.

"What was it captain?" the man asked. "Pirates or spirits?"

Hoff looked up at the sky, searching for the silhouette of his cargo ship among the stars. He wondered if what he had experienced was real. The shadowy figure of a young man, the icy air, the raven. It was like something from a terrible dream.

"Hoff?"

Hoff turned to his men. "You piles of pig vomit! You let pirates steal my ship!"

Hoff spent the rest of the night lying to his men about what had happened and believing his own stories.

SIX

S ORREN EXAMINED the long cut near his shoulder on his flesh-and-blood arm. The wound did not look deep; the trails and smears of dried blood underneath made it look worse than it actually was. The airship's owner had been a lousy swordsmen, and the sword hadn't been very sharp. The wound stung, but he was more annoyed about the sleeve of his coat being ruined.

Sorren had flown the airship above the mountains and set it on a slow course northward. He and Kovola were sitting in the airship's cargo room, now empty save for a few wobbly wooden chairs, a narrow wooden table, a log book full of schedules and statistics, and writing supplies. Sorren's staff stood leaning in a corner near a softly glowing lantern. Quove sat perched on the staff, facing his master.

"You let him slash you with a sword?" Kovola asked.

"It's only a small wound." Sorren squeezed the wound between his mechanical silver-copper fingers, testing the strength of the clotted blood. Red beads of fresh blood emerged and oozed down over his skin.

Kovola grimaced. "Even so," he said, "why wouldn't you disarm him first?"

"I wanted to see what he would do."

"What if he had stabbed you in the heart?" Kovola asked.

"Are you genuinely worried," Sorren said, "or are you trying to make a point?"

"Both."

Sorren wiped his mechanical hand on his shirt. "I'm not going to die by a sword." The wound was not likely to leave a permanent scar, but he didn't have the supplies to treat it properly. All he could do for now was go back to the caverns and clean the wound as best he could. "Where'd you put the mirror?"

Kovola thought for a moment, then stood up and started toward the door. "Left it in the engine room."

"You installed the lucator already?" Sorren asked, pulling his torn and blood-stained sleeve back down over his arm.

Kovola turned back and nodded. "I hope I did it right."

"Let me check," Sorren said. He put his hands on the table and slowed his breath. If the lucator was working properly, he'd be able to find it with his mind. It would feel like a weight somewhere in his subconscious, like some small inner voice crying out for attention. It was just a matter of letting all other thoughts float away. It didn't take long. Sorren caught it in his mind's eye and activated it, letting a portion of his Nyrish power flow into it. Not only would this eliminate the airship's need for fuel, it would also allow Sorren to, in a sense, *feel* the airship, to feel what it was doing and whether or not it was damaged. It made him and the airship *connected*.

Kovola shuddered. "Found it?"

Sorren let out his breath and nodded. "It's working."

"Good," Kovola said. "Let me get the mirror." He turned and left.

While Kovola went off to fetch the mirror, Sorren made his way across the hall to the navigation room. He ruffled through the pages of a journal he had left there earlier and studied a map of the kingdom he had drawn inside. He took a fountain pen from his pocket and wrote out some quick calculations, then adjusted some dials on the airship's control panels, rerouting the airship's course slightly eastward. He knew there was someone in the Takotoa Forest who could heal his arm quickly.

Back in the cargo room, Kovola placed the mirror on the table. Sorren whistled Quove to his shoulder and took his staff from the corner. Enchanting the mirror only took a few minutes, and the image of Thale appeared. He was sitting on the cavern's cold stone floor before the mirror, his head hidden by the large covers of a thick musty old book. Sorren's silver pocket watch sat at his side.

Sorren leaned over the mirror. "Thale."

Thale gasped and jerked backward, dropping the book from his hands. *Thud.* "Sorren. You scared me."

"How long?"

Thale glanced at the pocket watch. "Half an hour."

"That long?"

"Ooh." Thale flinched, leaning back. "Your arm."

"It's not as bad as it looks."

Kovola peered down at Thale through the mirror. "Have you been studying?"

"Yes," Thale said. "I'm tired of reading. When am I going to actually . . ." He wriggled his fingers. "I want to *do* something."

"It will take time," Kovola said. "We don't have a laboratory at the moment. It makes things difficult. And you still do not understand some of the basic theories."

Thale looked down at the book before him, his tovocular eye twisting back into his socket, and he sighed. "I know."

"Do you want to see the Ashwood Mountains?" Sorren asked.

Thale looked up. "What?"

"The skies are clear and the moons are bright," Sorren said, motioning for Thale to crawl through the portal with his silver-copper hand. "The kingdom is glowing."

Thale leaned forward and crawled through the portal as if he were climbing up through the table. After sliding over the table's edge, he looked around, studying the small dark room as if it were some new castle, his tovocular eye whirring in and out. "I've never been on an airship before."

"The best view of the mountains is from the navigation room windows, through there." Sorren pointed out the door. "Across the hall. Careful not to touch any controls."

"Where are we going?" Thale asked.

"Takotoa Forest."

"Is the Chosen One there?" Thale asked.

Kovola grunted. "Takotoa Forest? Are we going to see . . ."

His shoulders dropped and he rubbed the back of his neck. "Oh, please, Sorren, not him."

"I need his help," Sorren said, lifting his staff and dropping it through the mirror on the table. "I'm going to go wash up."

"You know he doesn't much care for you," Kovola said.

"Who does?" Sorren held out a hand for Quove. The raven flew to it, and Sorren dipped the hand down through the portal.

Kovola scoffed. "What makes you think he'll help you?"

"I'll ask him to." Sorren leaned forward and sunk headfirst into the mirror and into the caverns on the other side of the kingdom.

Kovola peered down through the portal and watched as Sorren stood up on the other side and disappeared into the shadows of the cavern. Then the old man flicked back his scraggly dark green hair and turned to Thale.

"Listen," Kovola said, "I know you've never been on an airship before, so enjoy it tonight. But from now on, it would be safer for you to stay in the caverns."

"Why?"

Kovola shook his head and looked back through the portal, silent, as if he didn't know what to say. Thale waited.

Finally, Kovola gestured at the portal and spoke softly. "Sorren doesn't . . . Sorren is . . . I'm not sure he understands what he's doing, what sort of dangers he's playing with. He just lost his father. His home. His future. You saw the cut on his arm. There was no reason for that to happen. He's exploring the edges of his talents. I know he's always been a bit brazen, reckless with his power, but his father was always there to . . . He listened to his father. And now, having lost so much, maybe he feels like he has nothing left to lose . . . I can no longer guess what he is becoming." Kovola put a hand on Thale's shoulder and spoke slowly. "Be careful."

SEVEN

ORNING WAS TURNING to noon as a small crowd gathered around Atlorus and Gashdane. An old woman stood before them, wrapped in a tattered brown shawl, recounting the miseries of village life she'd known under Vonlock's rule.

"His guards came at the end of every season and stole half our harvest. Our children starved. Our numbers have dwindled. We weren't even allowed to build churches. We gathered anyway. We gathered at night in the hills and we prayed." The old woman looked at Atlorus. She seemed to smile with only her eyes. "You are the answer to twenty-five years of prayers. The gods themselves have sent you."

Gashdane put an arm around the woman's shoulders. She seemed so frail, as if she might crumple in on herself like old paper. "We'll send food," Gashdane said. "And builders. And clothes and supplies and medicines. What Vonlock took from your village . . . from you . . . it will all be repaid tenfold."

The old woman put a hand to her mouth and wept.

Much of the morning had been like this. Atlorus and Gashdane, followed by a handful of Gashdane's Zolen soldiers, were exploring the small villages along Morrowgrand's southern coasts, listening to the stories of the people. Gashdane had insisted this sort of touring was necessary to gain the kingdom's trust. Gashdane would embrace the villagers and promise them a new beginning. If they were not overly emotional, Atlorus would promise to remember them and shake their hands. Sometimes they would bow to him as if he were already a king.

It felt strange to be so highly praised. What if he couldn't live up to their expectations? What if defeating Vonlock was the last remarkable thing he'd ever do? Of course, he could hardly ask these questions to anyone. So many people had suffered living in the shadow of a dark wizard for so long. Anything they had of value had been taken from them. Under Vonlock and his elite guards, they had lived like slaves. They needed hope. How could Atlorus deny them that? He would do whatever he could to help them.

Wiping tears from her face, the old woman walked forward and gently put her arms around Atlorus, her shawl smelling of dirt and mildew. Atlorus didn't care. With her warm hands pressed against his back, he thought of his mother. For a short moment, he was four years old again, gazing up at her, the sun and the summer trees behind her. Was she still there now?

The old woman kissed his head and mumbled what sounded like a prayer in a foreign language, then slowly walked away, becoming part of the small crowd. Several people bowed to Atlorus. Some made slow circles in the air with their hands, a rare blessing among them. Children stared at him as if they'd never seen anything so wondrous before and never would again.

Atlorus nodded, but could hardly stand to even make eye contact with them, looking to the clouds along the horizon behind them instead. He didn't deserve such praise. As the crowd began giving voice to some song of peace, Atlorus waved and turned back to the airship.

"The dark reign has ended!" Gashdane was still speaking to the crowds, his voice bellowing over their song. "A new world is coming! It has just been born! A new Morrowgrand!"

Atlorus owed a lot to Gashdane. It was Gashdane who had guided Atlorus from his home and instilled him with the courage necessary to fulfill the prophecy. It was Gashdane's faith in him that had saved Morrowgrand.

THERE WERE MANY ROOMS on Vonlock's royal airship. Bedrooms and ballrooms and libraries and lounges. It had been designed for luxury. Now Atlorus, Gashdane, and a small group of Zolen soldiers had the entire airship to themselves and were living like royalty.

Atlorus had taken the second largest bedroom for himself. The largest bedroom had most likely belonged to Vonlock, and Atlorus would not have been comfortable sleeping in a bedroom that once belonged to the darkest wizard to ever exist. He didn't believe in ghosts, but he believed in lingering memories, shadows that took time to fade. Anyway, the second bedroom was luxurious enough. A wide canopy bed sat in the center, small tables at its side, a bookshelf overflowing with treatises on wizardry and tove-crafting, a large wardrobe filled mostly with white shirts and long dark coats, and a large bureau with long rows of drawers. After having been raised in tiny forest huts and random mountain caverns, just this one room seemed like a palace.

Atlorus took a key from his pocket and unlocked a bureau drawer. Good. It was still there. The weapon he had used to defeat Vonlock. The weapon only he could use because he was the Chosen One. Somehow, checking that it was in place put Atlorus at ease. It was as if he and the weapon had become connected, as if they were part of each other. He needed to look upon it now and then to keep sane.

A voice whispered his name.

"Atlorus . . ."

Atlorus froze. He kept a hand hovering over the weapon as he slowly glanced around the room.

He was alone.

The whisper came again. "Atlorus . . ." It sounded distant, and Atlorus wondered if it was only in his head. He continued scanning the room for any sign of life.

Then he noticed it. A small mirror beside his bed had turned black. Completely black. Atlorus cautiously made his way toward it, leaving his weapon in the drawer. The mirror wasn't just black. There was a man inside. An old man with a long silvery beard, staring right through the glass at Atlorus.

"Atlorus," the old man said, leaning forward. "Is that you, Atlorus?"

Atlorus couldn't speak. His voice was stuck in his throat. He tried to swallow, but couldn't.

The old man smiled and waved a hand dismissively. "No reason to be scared of me, young master. You are Atlorus, the Chosen One. I cannot hurt you."

Atlorus turned to the bedroom door, ready to race away and find Gashdane.

"No no no, don't go!" the old man pleaded. "I have something to tell you! You are in great danger!"

Atlorus turned back, meeting the old man's wide-eyed gaze, and finally found his voice. "Danger?"

The old man nodded. "You are being hunted, young master. Forgive me for channeling you through a mirror. I had to warn you."

"Who are you?" Atlorus asked, inching toward the mirror.

"I am called Mordock," the old man said. "I am a wizard of the Nyrish Council."

The Nyrish Council? They were dark wizards, wizards who drew their powers from the Nyrish moon and frequently used it to rule over others. Vonlock had been part of the Nyrish Council, hadn't he?

"Some would call me a dark wizard, it's true," Mordock said, as if reading his thoughts. "But do not be so quick to judge all wizards of the Nyrish power by the cruelty of Vonlock. We were victims of his tyranny too. We did not have the strength to overthrow him ourselves. You have saved more than a kingdom. That is why I am indebted to you. And why I feel I must help you now."

Atlorus took slow breaths, trying to let himself relax. "You said I was being hunted?"

"There were two dark wizards in Vonlock's castle," Mordock said. "Vonlock and his son. Did you see Sorren?"

Atlorus nodded. "We saw each other across a hall. Near the staircase that leads to the throne room. He didn't even try to stop us. He just stood there watching."

"You let him live?"

Atlorus shook his head. "The Zolen soldiers threw bombs. Hand bombs. Devil's breath. We were using them against the guards." Atlorus held up a hand, mimicking holding the weight of a small bomb. "He deflected them. With a spell, I guess. But the explosions broke one of the thirty foot statues on the side of the staircase. It fell right on him and the stone just crumbled." Atlorus shuddered at the memory. It was like something from a nightmare. It was the look on Sorren's face as the statue fell on him. No fear, no remorse, no anger, as though his impending death meant nothing to him. "He was crushed by stone."

Mordock's gaze had somehow grown colder. "No," the old man said. "Sorren did not die that night."

Atlorus wasn't sure how to respond. How could anyone have survived what had happened to Sorren?

"Sorren lives," Mordock continued, "and his mind is consumed by one thing: avenging his father. He is hunting you, Atlorus, every hour of every day."

Atlorus thought this should make him afraid, but somehow the news didn't affect him. It was like something from a story or a dream, something distant and unreal.

"Of course, you shouldn't worry," Mordock said. "You defeated Vonlock. You can defeat Sorren too. Just be on your guard. He *will* find you. And it will probably be soon."

"How do you know this?" Atlorus asked.

"I have seen him," Mordock said. "I have seen him make an oath of blood to defeat you. I do not have the power to contend with him. You are the only one who does."

Atlorus sat in silence for a while, imagining ways in which Sorren might burst into his room. He'd have to keep his weapon close by at all times from now on. There would be no rest until Sorren joined his father.

"That is all I can tell you," Mordock said. "I am risking a lot by giving you this message. If Sorren finds out . . . But never-mind that. It is worth the risk. It is *you* I put my faith in, At-lorus. You face great trials for one so young, but you will do great things, I know. I must go now. Break your mirror when I am gone. It was enchanted by Vonlock himself, and I do not know how many other mirrors it may share enchantments with."

And then the old man disappeared, and Atlorus sat staring at himself. After a moment, he took the mirror and smashed it against the table's edge. Then he took the weapon from the drawer and held it tightly, promising to keep it close.

EIGHT

IT TOOK TWO DAYS for the small cargo airship to reach the Takotoa Forest. It would've taken longer if the airship had been running on ordinary fuel, but now that it was running on Sorren's Nyrish power, it could fly twice as fast. Being connected to the ship through his power, Sorren could sense the ship's speed throughout his body. It was as if it made his heart pump differently.

It was dusk when Sorren brought the ship to a fixed-float near the edge of the forest. He and Kovola descended from the ship's loading bay and walked into the forest, the green flame of Sorren's staff lighting the way. Kovola held a compass and a small map torn from a book, and he pointed his dark iron staff in the direction he thought they should go.

Sorren had wanted to bring Thale along. His tovocular eye would've been useful in the darkness. But Kovola had insisted that Thale needed to stay in the caverns and study from some other old thick musty book with fading ink. Sorren felt a bit sorry for him. Training to be a tove maker had to be one of the most boring adventures in the world.

Quove seemed to enjoy flying ahead of them, hopping from branch to branch, every now and then swooping down to catch some snack on the forest floor, an insect or a small mouse. Sometimes the raven vanished from sight completely, but Sorren knew she wouldn't wander off too far.

They finally came to a small round cottage with a yellow door. Its windows glowed with firelight and thick gray smoke bellowed from a chimney in the center of its roof.

Kovola folded up the small map. "This must be him." He shoved the map and compass into a pocket.

Sorren walked forward and tapped on the door with his staff.

Footsteps. Latches being unlatched. The door creaked open, only a bit, revealing half a face, a tall man in his late-twenties with a mess of brown hair and a pair of rectangular spectacles. He squinted. "Sorren?"

"Sage."

Sage stared at him for a moment, making no movement. Sorren stared back.

"Thought you were dead," Sage said.

"Can I come in?" Sorren asked.

Sage didn't open the door. "How did you survive?"

"He almost died," Kovola said, stepping forward. "Took me forever to find him. He was buried in stone. Lost his arm."

Sage's eyes went to Sorren's mechanical arm. He flung the door open and motioned the two inside. "Come in, come in."

The room inside was a mess. Wooden tables and chairs

were scattered around, the tables piled with books and junk. The walls were lined with shelves that overflowed with random trinkets, books, scrolls, and bottles of strange foreign ingredients, sands and powders and liquids of every color. It was not a home of luxury. Potions were Sage's specialty, and he apparently dedicated every waking moment to his work. A strange smell filled the place, at once both sweet and putrid, like a mix of warm cinnamon bread and a sweaty man's dirty shoes. A wide circular hearth sat in the middle of the room, the chimney hovering over it. The entire room baked in the orange light of its roaring fire.

Sage grabbed Sorren's silver-copper arm, pushed back his sleeve, and brought it close to his eyes as if it were some puzzle to be solved. His eyes went up and down the length of the arm and he poked his fingers between the silver rods that formed the forearm. "Very impressive," he said. "Your work is a bit sloppy at the wrist, though. And why didn't you give yourself additional fingers?"

Sorren tore his arm from Sage's grip and showed him the wound on his other arm. "Do you have something for this? I don't want a scar."

Sage grabbed this arm too and squeezed it. "Does this hurt?"

"Yes," Sorren said, again pulling himself from Sage's grip. "What are you doing?"

"Sit down," Sage said. "It will take me half an hour to make it."

Kovola was carefully clearing books from a chair near the hearth. "Make what?" he asked.

"Treethrice glue," Sage said, walking to some shelves and filling his arms with seemingly random things. A vial of liquid here, a jar of sand there, a wilting flower here, a box of seeds there. "It'll accelerate skin growth, keep the sides of the cut together, and won't leave a scar." He paused and looked at Sorren with squinted eyes. "It will also be extremely, tremendously, remarkably painful."

Sorren ignored the comment, leaned his staff against a chair, and browsed some of the old books on the tables. *The Game of Gynwig, The Book of the Harbinger, How to Make Music Boxes, Moonrise Ink and other Forbidden Tales.* They seemed to be random. History books and how-to books and storybooks and song books.

Sage had been Sorren's tutor years ago, from when Sorren was seven years old to ten years old, teaching him everything he could about history, mathematics, potions, and the arts. They were the only formal lessons Sorren had ever received. Though Vonlock had paid him very well, Sage eventually quit, angry that Sorren rarely gave him his full attention and never did his assignments. It was true that Sorren hated the lessons, but he still missed Sage after he left. He hoped the past would not come up in their conversations.

Sage set his supplies down on a table. "Read a book. This will take time." He set about creating the potion, mixing things and heating things and timing things.

Kovola sat near the hearth, browsing through scrolls of some sort, frowning as if he disapproved of everything he read.

Sorren sat at a table and rummaged through some other books, finally settling on an old book of children's tales called

Maker of the Twenty-first Moon. He remembered reading the title story years ago, perhaps out of this very same book when Sage had been at the castle. He reread it now, slowly, contemplating every sentence as if the story was full of secrets. The story was the same he remembered, but the spirit of the story had somehow changed. It involved a father dying for his son, and his son vowing revenge. When he had read it years ago, it somehow felt like fun entertainment. Now it was a devastatingly serious tragedy. Though he knew he was very different, Sorren felt a close connection to the child in the story, the child left fatherless at the end. It was almost as if his own life was being written by the same storyteller. But he knew his own story would end differently.

"That bird has been staring at me since before you arrived," Sage said.

Sorren looked up and followed Sage's eyes to a window across the room. Quove sat on the other side of the window, staring in.

"It's Quove," Sorren said.

"You still have that bird? Do you want to let her in?"

"She'll be fine," Sorren said. "She just likes to keep a watch on things."

"She looks like she wants to gouge out my eyes."

"She probably does."

"The treethrice glue is done."

Kovola stood up and looked at the small steaming bowl sitting in front of Sage. "That's treethrice glue?"

"Yes."

"Is it hot?"

"Very." Sage stood up, took the bowl, grabbed a paintbrush from the table, and walked toward Sorren. "As I told Sorren here, this will be extremely, dreadfully, horrendously painful. But it won't a leave a scar."

Sorren slid out of his coat, resting it on the back of his chair, and pulled up his sleeve. He held out a hand to take the brush. "I can do it."

"*I* will do it," Sage said. "This requires the steady practiced hands of a master." He pulled a chair next to Sorren, facing his wounded arm. "But first, another sensitivity test. It's very important." He pressed his thumb against the wound, digging it in as if trying to reopen the cut. Pain shot through Sorren's entire shoulder and down through his arm. He held his breath, resisting the urge to shout.

Sage took his thumb away with a hint of a smile and Sorren gasped, catching his breath.

"Was that really necessary?" Kovola asked.

"Oh, yes," Sage said. "Very important. You see, it gets the heart pounding. Good for blood flow."

Sorren couldn't tell whether or not he was lying.

"And if you thought that hurt," Sage said, stirring the brush in the thick dark green steaming liquid, "then you don't know real pain at all." He pulled the brush out, let it drip for a moment, then quickly slathered it across Sorren's wound. It was as if someone held a flaming torch to his skin. His heart raced, his fists tightened, his mechanical arm began to shake, sweat trickled down the side of his head, and he clenched his teeth.

"Oh dear," Sage said. "Should've given you something to bite down on. Sorry about that." He continued slathering on the green glue, globs of it rolling down the sides of Sorren's arm and dripping onto the floor.

Sorren closed his eyes, trying to concentrate, letting his mind forget the present moment, trying to find some calm memory, some peaceful place his heart remembered. But all he saw in his mind's eye was the Chosen One's face, staring at him from across a castle hall. And then the Chosen One and the soldiers behind him were tossing hand bombs his way. And then the statue was falling. The grand figure of his great great great grandfather who had been king over a century ago. It had happened in slow motion. The bottom of the stone figure cracked, then the legs began to crumble, and the top half of the body turned to the side as if to look at Sorren, tumbling face-first toward him.

"Done," Sage said.

Sorren opened his eyes, panting, wiping sweat from his head with his mechanical arm. The burning sensation was fading. Now it felt only like a splash of melted candle wax.

"You'll be healed in seven days," Sage said, standing up and walking to the fire in the center of the room. "Until then, don't scratch the wound. Drink plenty of liquids, get plenty of sleep, and most importantly, whatever you do, don't . . . uh . . . do not, um . . . I can't remember."

Sorren blew on the wound, trying to cool it off.

Sage looked down at the bowl and brush in his hands. "Can't use these anymore." He tossed them into the fire, which sparkled and crackled and sent a burst of red flame up into the chimney before settling back to normal. "Now then," he said, turning back to Sorren and Kovola, "we must discuss payment."

"Payment?" Kovola repeated.

"My ingredients were not cheap," Sage said. "It is only fair that I am reimbursed for my expenses. And my time."

Sorren stood up. "I'm not going to pay you," he said.

"You have to."

"No, I don't," Sorren said, taking his staff in his silver-copper hand and slowly turning it.

Sage stared at the staff. "Are you threatening me?"

"Do you feel threatened?"

Sage stared at Sorren and scratched his chin for a short moment. "No."

"Good," Sorren said. "I have nothing to pay you with."

"Yes, you do," Sage said, walking to a table on the other side of the room, "or I would never have let you in." He picked up a journal, opened it, and held it out for Sorren to see, showing a mess of scribbly notes and diagrams. "For the past year, I've been studying the moons. The Nyrish moon especially. There's more than just light flowing from it. It's sending down some other kind of energy."

Sorren couldn't understand any of Sage's notes. His handwriting was so sloppy that it looked like a foreign language. "So what do you want from me?"

"Your power."

"I can't give you that."

"I mean *access* to your power. I want to make some measurements while you're enchanting something or casting a spell."

Seemed easy enough. "How long will it take?" Sorren

asked.

"A few months."

"What?"

"I need multiple measurements for each and every phase of the moons," Sage said. "Also, I need to do it all over again in the summer because the tilt of the planet changes."

"I don't have time," Sorren said, picking up his coat and draping it over his arm. "Maybe next year."

Sage closed the journal. "Don't have time? Are you running from Atlorus?"

"I'm not running from Atlorus."

"Quite the contrary," Kovola said. "He's trying to *find* Atlorus."

Sage looked confused. "Is this true?"

Sorren picked up the book he had read just a short while ago, *Maker of the Twenty-first Moon.* "Can I have this?"

"Why are you trying to find Atlorus?" Sage asked.

Sorren tucked the book under his arm. "I have to defeat him so that I can become Head of the Nyrish Council."

"Ah," Sage said, nodding as if he now understood some grand truth. "Of course. How hard could that be?"

Sorren turned to leave.

"Have you even read the prophecy?" Sage called out behind him. "Do you know what the Candlewood Prophecy actually states?"

Sorren paused and turned around. Truth was, he had no idea what exactly the prophecy stated.

Sage quickly rummaged through a bottom shelf on a far wall. "Here we are," he said, returning to the table with a thin book bound in fading blue leather. "*Maewyn's Book of Prophecies, Volume Seven.*" He sat down and began leafing through the pages. "Granted, most of these *are* nonsense, the delusions of dying madmen. Such as the invisible dragon prophecy. Invisible dragons will eat everyone's first born son for a hundred years. That one won't keep me up at night. But the Candlewood Prophecy. Here." He ran his hand down the length of a page near the back of the book.

Sorren peered over the table, trying to make out the text.

"It's written in Old Tavendin," Sage said, "which I know you can't read because you have no patience for learning languages. My Tavendin needs work, but, roughly translated, the prophecy states: 'A tower that rises too close to the stars cannot bear its own weight, and collapses in the wind. So it is with the power of the Candlewood family. For seven generations, the family's branches will wither and die. On the eleventh day of the eleventh month, the moons will send forth the final destroyer. He will be born under the very shadow he will destroy, and he will vanquish the last of the Candlewood family. He will become king and lead his kingdom out of the darkness. Never again will one suffer at the hands of the Candlewood family's power.' It's dated about two hundred fifty years ago."

"That doesn't really tell me anything," Sorren said.

Sage took off his spectacles and rubbed his eyes. "Don't you realize you're a part of this?" he asked. "The Candlewood Prophecy has not yet been fulfilled. The Chosen One has one last wizard to kill."

Sorren gazed at the book and whispered the seizing spell in his mind, sending the book into his hand. He couldn't read the language, but the prophecy seemed rather short compared to the other ones.

"You're the last of the Candlewood family, Sorren," Sage said. "The prophecy calls for your death."

"And you're walking *toward* it," Kovola added.

Sage slid his spectacles back on his nose, pressing the bridge between his eyes. "I don't believe prophecies are mystical things," he said. "Most men and women who call themselves prophets are deluding themselves, it's true. But there are a few people who find themselves in tune with . . ." He waved his arms around at his side. "They're not getting messages from mystical dimensions or unexplainable dreams. They're just in tune with things. They can sense things. A bit like how some animals can sense when a storm is coming. They can see things other people can't and draw conclusions from them. Whoever wrote this prophecy must have known something, must have sensed something about the Candlewood family that he or she knew would eventually lead to its downfall."

Sorren snapped the book shut and tossed it across the table. "There's only one way to find out if it's true."

Sage dropped his head to the table like an upset child.

"He won't listen to anyone," Kovola said.

"An *eleven year old* killed the most powerful Wizard King in the *world*," Sage said, "and you think it might be chance?"

"I have a long distance to fly tonight," Sorren said, turning back toward the door.

"Wait," Sage said. "Let me come with you."

"What?" Kovola said. "Why?"

"I'd like to make *some* measurements before the last of the Candlewood family dies."

"Come, then," Sorren said, walking toward the door. "You can fly the airship."

NINE

THAT NIGHT, Sorren, Kovola, and Sage flew the small airship southward to the Thornblack Mountains. They were the tallest mountains in Morrowgrand, and stood next to a long wide valley called Thornwood Pass. The pass was a common route taken by airships; the valley was little more than a vast expanse of grasses, and the Thornblack Mountains shielded the valley from cold ocean winds. It was the smoothest sailing one could find in the kingdom.

Sailing was not so smooth beside the lofty mountain peaks, which almost pierced the clouds. The winds were wild and wicked up here, and the eastern ocean's cold breath rushed through the control room's broken window. But Sorren wanted the ship floating far above the pass so that they'd have the best vantage point from which to search the distant landscapes for his father's royal airship. From such a grand height, the kingdom seemed to stretch on for miles and miles, glowing in the pale blue moonlight. Patches of distant farmland looked like strange quilt work, entire forests looked like stubble, and the stone buildings of distant villages looked like the toys of a child.

There they waited, gazing through the windows, scanning the skies below for any sign of Vonlock's royal airship.

Vonlock's airship would be over ten times the length of the cargo airship, and over five times the height. It would be painted a rich shade of blue, the color of the Nyrish moon, and its thick trails of steam would be visible from great distances. It had been built to look imposing, to cast long shadows and remind the kingdom who was king. Sorren imagined the Chosen One walking its wide halls and sleeping in its majestic bedrooms. He imagined the the boy going through his father's things, going through his own things. Sorren didn't want any of it back. It was all a memorial to another life now.

Neither Sorren nor Sage nor Kovola spotted anything that night. They used the mirror to retire to the caverns, and the next night they returned to the airship to continue the search. Still nothing.

On the third night, the winds were much calmer, and Sorren was tired of searching.

I need Thale, he thought, staring through the front windows of the navigation room, standing behind Sage who sat at the ship's control panel.

Kovola was gazing through the side windows. Sorren could hardly tell if he was still searching the skies, or if his mind had drifted into a daydream. The old man would not want Sorren bringing Thale here. Sorren didn't feel like arguing with him.

He shook his mechanical arm. "Bah," he said, pretending to

have trouble wriggling his fingers. "Hand's getting stiff."

"I told you," Sage said, "your work is sloppy. You'll have to rebuild that whole thing from scratch."

"Just needs oil," Sorren said, turning to leave the room. "Kovola, I'm going to borrow your ventor's oil." It was oil Kovola used for tove-making. Sorren knew it was one of the supplies he had managed to escape the castle with.

"Wait," Kovola said, following Sorren out of the navigation room.

Sorren ignored him, walking to the storage room near the back of the airship. He tapped the tip of his staff against the small mirror on the table. His reflection faded away, revealing an empty cavern room, torches lighting its cool damp walls.

"I'll get it," Kovola said, putting a hand on Sorren's shoulder. "I don't want you using the rest of it. I don't have much left."

"We can get more," Sorren said, leaning over the portal, preparing to slide through.

Kovola clutched Sorren's coat and pulled him back. "Sorren, I said *I* would get it."

Sorren stood back and sighed, brushing a hand through his hair.

Kovola climbed on the table and carefully slid his legs through the mirror. "I'll be back in a moment."

Sorren watched as Kovola climbed through the portal and disappeared into the shadows of the caverns beyond.

Good. His plan had worked perfectly. Kovola was out of the way.

Sorren put a finger to his throat and thought a small enchantment, a spell that would carry his whisper to its one intended listener. "Thale." The whisper echoed through the cavern halls like a chorus of ghosts.

Moments later, Thale crept into the cavern room, peering around.

Sorren, looking down through the portal, beckoned the boy forward. "Thale. I need your help."

Thale approached the mirror. "My help?"

"I still can't find my father's airship."

Thale took a step back and bit his lip. "Kovola's making me read more books."

"This won't take long."

"Is Kovola there?"

"He's back in the caverns somewhere," Sorren said. "He's getting something for me."

Thale looked back into the shadows behind him, as though unsure about something. Then he turned back to Sorren and extended a hand. "Help me up."

Sorren held out his silver-copper hand and pulled Thale up through the mirror. As Thale made his way out of the storage room, Sorren pointed his staff at the mirror and whispered an enchantment to close the portal. The caverns slowly vanished, and Sorren's reflection appeared. That would keep Kovola out of the way for a bit.

Sorren followed Thale into the navigation room.

"My father's airship," Sorren said, nodding toward the front windows. "Can you see it?"

"Hmmm." Thale closed his human eye and leaned forward, the lens of his tovocular eye protruding from his socket like an extending spyglass, faintly buzzing.

Sage looked up over his shoulder. He didn't say anything, but he was obviously fascinated by Thale's eye, staring at it as if it were some fascinating treasure. Sorren almost expected him to reach out and grab it as he'd done with his own mechanical arm.

Thale's head slowly turned. "There's a lot of kingdom out there. Is your father's airship flying?"

"How well can you see the moons?" Sage asked.

"Don't worry about the moons right now," Sorren said. "The airship may be airborne, or on the ground near a village. Atlorus is touring the kingdom. That's all I know."

Thale's eye whirred, twisting in and out of his socket. Sorren knew the boy's eye could see farther than even a sea captain's longest spyglass, and the darkness would be no obstacle for it.

After a few minutes, Thale sighed. "This'll take time." He pulled his tovocular eye out, scratched the inner rim of his now empty eye socket, and rubbed the lens of his eye on his sleeve.

Sage stood up and squirmed between Sorren and Thale to the back of the room. "Sit down then," he said. "I've been sitting all night."

Thale took the empty seat and rested his chin on his knuckles, putting a hand over his human eye.

Hours went by. Sorren and Sage eventually retreated to the navigation room floor, sitting with their backs against the wall. Sage was busy sketching something in his small journal, while Sorren polished his silver-copper hand with a small cloth.

Kovola must be furious, Sorren thought. By now he must have discovered that Thale wasn't in the caverns and that the portal had been closed. Sorren wondered what the old man would do. Kovola was not the sort of person who shouted or threw tantrums when he was angry. But then, Sorren had never tricked him like this before.

"I've got it," Thale said, his eye whirring about.

Sorren and Sage stood up.

"Where?" Sorren asked, leaning forward.

Thale pointed two fingers slightly leftward. "The ship's flying low, over those forests."

"Owl's Fortress?" Sage said, squinting.

Owl's Fortress was a long stretch of forested hills near Morrowgrand's eastern coasts, named for the great variety of owls they gave home to. From the cargo ship's grand height, they were just a stretch of bumpy landscape to the naked eye.

"There are no towns or villages near Owl's Fortress," Sage said. "Why would they be flying around there?"

"Are you sure it's my father's airship?" Sorren asked.

"I'm certain," Thale said. "Just a black dot with my real eye, but I can see it perfectly with my other."

"Owl's Fortress then," Sorren said. He tapped Thale on the shoulder. "Let Sage fly."

Thale left the seat and Sage took it, putting his hands on the helm. "You want to fly there now?"

"The Chosen One is on that ship," Sorren said.

"It'll take hours from where we are," Sage said.

Sorren glanced out the broken window on the side and looked up at the Nyrish moon, floating brightly in the western skies. It was almost a half moon tonight. The more full it was, the more Nyrish power a Nyrish wizard could collect from it. A half moon would be enough.

"It won't take hours," Sorren said. "It'll take minutes."

"Owl's Fortress is way over there," Sage said, pointing ahead. "We can barely even see it from here. That's a long distance."

"Yes, it is," Sorren said.

Sage sat in silence for a moment. "Ah," he said. "You installed something on the engine? *You're* powering the ship?"

"I am."

Sage shook his head. "It's still too far. It'll take us at least half an hour."

"Just fly," Sorren said. "I'll worry about giving the ship the power it needs."

Sage grimaced.

"Give me a moment," Sorren said. He left and returned with the mirror from the storage room.

"Why do you need that?" Thale asked.

"Don't want it to break," Sorren said, holding the mirror out to Thale. "Do you want to go back?"

"Go back?"

"To the caverns."

Thale took the mirror and glanced at his reflection. "You closed the portal?"

"Yes," Sorren said.

"Why?"

Sorren didn't answer the question. "I can open it again. Do you want to go back?"

Thale only stared at the mirror, as if waiting for his reflection to answer for him.

Sorren turned to the broken window and whistled. "This airship is about to fly faster than the wind," he said. Quove flew through the broken window and landed on his shoulder. "And it will fly straight toward the Chosen One. This'll be dangerous."

Thale kept his eyes on his reflection. "Then why are you doing it?" he asked.

Sage glanced over his shoulder. "Atlorus took everything from him. His father. His kingdom. His castle."

Sorren shook his head and clenched his scepter in his flesh and blood hand, letting its grooves of cold iron press into his skin. He gazed out the front window and tried to imagine his father's airship somewhere down there, across the vast kingdom, being flown by the boy who killed his father. "Everyone is piling their hopes on a boy they barely know," Sorren said. "They think creating a new world is like lighting a candle. A burst of flame and it's done. But it's not. I'm changing everything."

Thale and Sage were silent.

After a few moments, Thale held the mirror tightly to his chest. "I won't let this break."

Sorren nodded. "Sit down, back and head against the wall." Thale obeyed, and Sorren turned to Sage, gripping the back of his chair. "Out of fixed-float. First gear. Fly."

Sage shivered and strapped himself to his seat. "Don't get too excited," he said, pulling switches on the control board. "It's cold enough in these mountains." He slowly turned the helm to the left while pushing a small lever on the control board, pointing the airship downward so that it was facing Owl's Fortress directly. Then he slowly pushed another lever, and the airship began flying forward.

"Keep steady," Sorren said, backing away from the control board and leaning against the back wall. Again he glanced out the broken window and up at the Nyrish moon, whispering some of the most basic spells known to wizards of the Nyrish power. Instantly, a warmth pervaded through him, through his blood, like a river of warm water pouring through his heart and lungs. It was the flow of the Nyrish power, always a peaceful and welcoming feeling, like meeting an old friend by a fireside after a long journey.

Sorren carefully directed the power to the part of his mind that held the airship and its engine. With that, the airship quaked as if in a storm and accelerated forward. Sorren let the force of the acceleration pull his arms to his side. The world outside the window seemed to warp slightly, smearing at the edges, and the mountains blurred past the windows. The wind became the sound of a waterfall, roaring like some incredible beast.

Sage groaned, leaning forward and clutching the helm as though his life depended on it. Thale had curled up against the wall with his chin against his chest, his eye closed tightly.

Sorren kept the airship tearing through the sky, feeling for the limits of what the old ship could handle with his mind. Too fast, and the ship might rip apart against the force the wind. But Sorren was not concerned about that. He could handle the flow of the Nyrish power. It was what waited for him above

Owl's Fortress that concerned him.

He'd be there soon. Only a few minutes more.

Then he would face Atlorus again. Then he would find out how the boy had killed his father.

TEN

SEVEN SECONDS before Gashdane knocked on his door, Atlorus woke up, half imagining he had heard his mother calling his name. It took him a moment to remember where he was and who he had become. When Gashdane knocked on the door, he was not surprised. It was as though some part of his mind had expected it.

"Yes?" Atlorus called out.

Gashdane entered the dark room holding a golden candelabrum. He took a candle from it and began lighting the lanterns along the wall, giving the room an amber glow. "I'm afraid you must wake," Gashdane said. "There's an airship following us. Only a cargo ship, but there are no trade routes around here. They must've recognized our ship. They must want to meet you."

"A cargo ship?" Atlorus said, sitting up. He still had his weapon clasped in his hand, a small black crystal. He could feel it pressing into his palm beneath his fingers. He opened his fist to make sure.

"Atlorus," Gashdane said slowly, as if he'd caught the boy stealing, "Atlorus, you shouldn't sleep with that."

Atlorus rolled the crystal between his fingers. "Why not?"

"It's dangerous. You don't know what a dream may do. You may activate it in sleep."

"I have to keep it close," Atlorus said.

Gashdane walked over to the end of the bed and shook his head. He spoke gently, as if trying to calm a child's nightmares. "That dark night is over. The dark wizard is gone. Don't let your memories haunt you. Don't keep shadows with you."

"No," Atlorus said, pulling off his covers and stepping out of bed. "It's not over."

"Atlorus . . ."

"It's Sorren," Atlorus said, pulling on a robe to keep him warm. "Son of the dark wizard. He's coming."

"Atlorus . . ."

"He's on that cargo ship. He's coming for me."

Gashdane sighed and looked at the floor. "You've seen a lot for one so young . . ."

Atlorus looked at Gashdane and waited for the man to return his gaze. When Atlorus said nothing, Gashdane looked up at him.

"I *know* it's Sorren," Atlorus said. "I . . ." He wasn't about to tell Gashdane that some other dark wizard had warned him through an enchanted mirror. That would only scare Gashdane. "I saw him in a dream. He survived that night."

"Only a dream . . ."

"No," Atlorus said. "I can *sense* him. It must be a part of my power." He held the black crystal in his palm. Only he could activate the weapon. That was the power of the Chosen One.

"We saw that statue smash him," Gashdane said. "We *saw* it with our own eyes."

"I know. But I can feel it with the beating of my heart." That was an expression his mother often used. *I can feel it with the beating of my heart.* "That night is always with me. I watch him being crushed every hour in my mind. But I can *feel* that he's near. I trust my heart more than my eyes."

"I suppose it's possible," Gashdane said, staring at the black crystal in Atlorus's hand. "Who can say how your power works? If Sorren lives, then the prophecy has not yet been fulfilled."

"It will be soon," Atlorus said, closing his fingers around the crystal. He had been terrified on the night he led Zolen soldiers into Vonlock's castle. But he trusted the black crystal now, and he trusted his own power. He had seen what they could do. There was no more fear. "Let him come."

ELEVEN

SORREN LET OUT a long breath. The small cargo airship was now flying behind and below his father's grand royal airship. It loomed overhead like an enormous storm cloud. Sage was trembling in his seat, his hands lightly resting on spokes of the helm, keeping the ship flying slow and straight. The exciting flight to Owl's Fortress had apparently agitated his nerves.

Thale had responded to the dangerous flight more stoically. When it was over, he had simply stood up and stared out the front window as though nothing interesting had happened. But he wouldn't look at Sorren.

"Now what?" Sage asked. "Are you going to blast fireballs at it?"

"I'm not going to destroy my father's ship," Sorren said. "*My* ship." His father was gone. The royal airship was *his* airship now, wasn't it? "There's a docking bay door on the back, between the steam vents. You'd see it easily in daylight."

"I can see it," Thale said, his tovocular eye twisting outward. "It's wide. Nearly the width of the ship."

"Yes," Sorren said. "Fly close to that and I'll open it."

"And then?" Sage asked.

"This whole ship should fit inside. It's a docking bay."

"Should?" Sage repeated. "And what if it doesn't?"

"Then we move on to plan B," Sorren said.

"And what's plan B?"

"Plan B is to think of another plan."

"I'm glad you know what you're doing," Sage said.

"I've never needed a plan B before," Sorren said. "Just keep flying."

Sage brought the cargo ship steadily closer to the gigantic ship above. His trembling hands settled a bit, but Sorren could tell he was still tense. His breathing was slow and labored.

"Uh oh," Sage said.

"What?" Sorren asked. But he knew the answer a second later. His father's airship was slowing down. There was no place for it to land; there were only forests below.

Sage gave voice to the same thought turning in Sorren's mind. "They know they're being followed."

"They can't know by who," Sorren said.

"By *whom*," Sage wisely corrected him.

Sorren ignored him. "The kingdom thinks I'm dead. Approach the docking bay door and see if they'll open it for us."

"They must be suspicious," Sage said. "This is no place for a cargo ship to be flying."

"Do you want to go back to the caverns?" Sorren asked. "I can fly myself."

"I have more experience," Sage said. "You need me."

As the royal airship above them came to stop in the air, Sage brought the cargo ship to a stop behind it, then slowly pulled back on the helm, guiding the ship upward.

"Look," Thale said. "They *are* opening the bay door."

Indeed, narrow strips of orange light outlined the edges of the wide rectangular door, slowly growing as the door opened outward.

"Convenient," Thale said.

"Too convenient," Sage said, bringing the cargo ship level with the bay door.

"Look inside, Thale," Sorren said. "Tell me what you see."

Thale put a hand over his human eye, and his tovocular eye whirled inward and outward. "There are people inside. Five or six. Zolen soldiers. They're . . . they're holding something . . ."

The door was almost completely open now, revealing the silhouettes of men standing in a row. Sage slowly sent the cargo ship forward.

"Wait!" Thale grabbed at Sage's arm.

Sage jumped in his chair. "What are you try—"

"Fly down!" Thale said. "They're throwing bo—"

Boom!

A low roar bellowed through the air, and the world beyond the window turned to fire, balls of flame curling in on one another. The cargo ship jolted downward and to the side, sending Sorren crashing up against the ceiling and the side wall, forcing all breath from his lungs. The sound of shattering glass rang in his ear. He clutched his staff and pulled himself back to his feet. Outside, the fireballs had turned into a thick cloud of smoke, impossible to see through.

"Thale," Sorren said between gasps, "can you see . . ."

Then Sorren noticed that Thale was sprawled against the floor, arms at his side. He was searching the floor as if he'd lost something. Sorren extended a hand to help the boy up, but something crunched under his foot. He slid his foot to the side. A shard of the mirror. The floor was covered in pieces of the shattered mirror.

Thale looked up at him, not taking his hand, his face pale as moonlight. "It broke," he said. "I couldn't hold it."

"Are you all right?" Sorren asked, reaching his silver-copper arm closer to him.

"I think so," Thale said, taking Sorren's hand and pulling himself up.

"Hold on to something," Sage said, scrambling with the controls before him. The cargo ship had come to a stop slightly below the opened bay door.

"Hold on to what?" Thale asked.

But Sage ignored the question and sent the ship lurching forward, under the royal airship. Sorren and Thale stumbled backward. The roar of more bombs bursting in air echoed somewhere behind them. The sounds shook the cargo ship's walls. Sorren's muscles throbbed as if his blood had turned to pudding. His connection with the ship was becoming painful. But he couldn't cut the connection. The blasts had damaged the engine. Sorren could feel it. Now it was only the flow of his power that kept the ship afloat.

"You didn't see a boy around your age back there," Sorren asked Thale, "did you?"

Thale shook his head. "Only Zolen soldiers."

Sorren put a hand on Sage's shoulder. "Fly to the front of the ship and turn and rise."

"What?" Sage asked.

"Bring the ships face to face," Sorren said, twisting his staff in his flesh-and-blood hand. "I will send them fire of my own." Then he clutched his staff in both hands and pointed it out the front window, trying to remember the words of the fire spells he had mastered years ago.

Sage nodded and pulled some levers at the control board. "By the way," he said. "I think they know you're alive."

It *was* odd that they had attacked an otherwise harmless cargo airship so quickly. Did they attack every suspicious airship like that? Or did they know Sorren himself was onboard? *It doesn't matter,* Sorren thought. *If they didn't know I was alive, they'll know it soon.*

Sage began reversing the cargo ship's orientation as it neared the head of the ship above. When they finally flew out from under the royal airship, Sage sent the cargo ship rising upward. The walls of the royal airship before them seemed to slowly descend, floor after floor of long rows of windows and balconies made for a king.

When the cargo ship rose to face the top deck, there he was. Atlorus, just as he had looked on the night he killed Sorren's father. He stood at the edge of the top deck, arms against a wide railing, staring straight at Sorren. A taller figure stood behind him, his face lost in shadow. Sorren guessed it to be Gashdane, head of the Zolen army.

"It's him," Thale said. "The Chosen One."

"Yes," Sorren said, gazing at the boy, willing the green flame of his staff to burn bright enough to almost blind the boy gazing back.

They stood there, staring at each other, Sorren in a stolen cargo airship, Atlorus on his father's royal airship.

On second thought, Sorren decided Atlorus did *not* look the same. His eyes were cold, his face was relaxed, his arms did not tremble. He was calm. He was no longer a coward. The way the moonlight struck his face reminded Sorren of a painting he might've seen in a dream.

Sorren kept the boy's gaze as he repositioned his hands on his staff, preparing to blast a stream of fire through the window, aiming at the railing below the boy's hands.

But as he did so, Atlorus slowly brought his left hand to his side, raising it behind his head and making a fist as if preparing to throw a punch.

"He's holding something," Thale said.

The tove that killed my father, Sorren thought.

Thale's eye spun madly as Atlorus flung his arm forward. "It looks like a small black cry—"

TWELVE

IT HAPPENED QUICKLY. It appeared above them like a hole in the world, a wide hole that twisted the world at its edges, forming a tunnel above them that led to nothingness, a vast and empty nothingness, a void blacker than the sky. Its edges seemed to shimmer, to pulsate, singing in tones both high and low like a crowd of children wailing in agony under the deafening roar of a crumbling mountain. The void was pulling the airship inside as if it were the throat of some starving beast seeking to devour all it saw. The winds cried through the walls.

Sorren's heart pounded in his ears. His connection with the airship was quickening his pulse, sending tremors through his limbs. He could feel the force of the dark vortex working to rip the ship apart, and he understood what he had to do.

Sorren closed his eyes, cut his connection with the airship as he might cut a rope with a knife, and went weightless. The choir of children seemed to fade into the distance. Sorren opened his eyes to find the hole shrinking back into the sky. It seemed to happen in slow motion. The cargo ship flipped backward, tumbling from the sky like a struck bird, dead and powerless without Sorren's power coursing through it. Sage was strapped in his seat, clutching at the helm, but Thale floated before the windows, twisting and flailing and grabbing at air. Beyond the window, the world was nothing but a blur of the forest trees below, turning, spinning, growing.

And then the windows shattered and all was darkness.

THIRTEEN

THE LIGHT WAS BLINDING. Sorren realized it was the sun flashing through the trees. What happened? Where was he? How long had he been unconscious?

He tried to sit up, but couldn't. His entire body was numb, stiff. He felt like a floating thought trapped in one place.

A blurry face appeared before him, looking down. Sorren tried to bring the vision into focus. It was a woman's face. An older woman, wrinkles beginning to form at the edges of her eyes and mouth. Perhaps it was a trick of the morning light, but the woman's pale skin almost seemed a faint shade of magenta. Her eyes were the deep blue of the Nyrish moon and, like the moon, they seemed to glow. A bundle of worn out wooden necklaces hung from her neck, clacking against one another. Thick strands of hair hung from her head, black with random strands of dark red and purple, long enough that they almost touched Sorren's face. They smelled of dirt and smoke.

The woman's voice was warm, smooth, peaceful as a summer sunrise over calm waters. "I am Maewyn," she said. "Welcome to Owl's Grave."

Sorren tried to respond, but could not find the strength. A darkness rose over him like a blanket, a warm welcoming darkness, and he let it swallow him.

FOURTEEN

"**S**ORREN," a voice whispered. It was faint and hard to hear, like something echoing from deep inside a cavern.

"Mordock," Sorren whispered into the shadows.

"Sorren," the voice repeated.

No, Sorren thought, *it's Kovola*. He struggled to find his way back to reality. "Kovola," he said, his voice weak.

"Sorren, are you there?"

"I'm here."

"Sorren? Are you awake?"

Sorren opened his eyes. A low ceiling made of sticks hovered above, lit by the flickering glow of a torch's flame. Sorren turned his head, relieved to have some ability to move again. Sage was kneeling beside him, squinting at him through his narrow spectacles like a scholar studying a rare book.

"Sage?" Sorren said.

"Awake now?" Sage asked. "Can you move yet? They gave

you some powerful medicines. Ankridge root and mirkglen powder. Rare ingredients. Even I don't work with those."

Sorren brought his mechanical hand before his face and tested the movement of his fingers. All seemed to function normally. Then he tested his flesh-and-blood hand, breathing warmth into his palm, making sure he could feel it. His flesh-and-blood hand trembled slightly, but it was hardly noticeable. A thin smell of incense was on the air.

Sorren noticed his coat draped over the footboard. Quove stood perched on it, staring back at him like a curious child. He tried to sit up, but his right leg was numb.

"You broke it," Sage said. "You should've seen it. It was twisted in a shape I didn't know was possible. It should heal though."

"Where's Thale?" Sorren asked.

"In another hut," Sage said. "He didn't fare so well. Broken arm, fractured ribs, internal injuries. Nasty. But he should heal too. At least, I hope so."

"Hope so?" Sorren pushed himself up with his arms and studied his leg. Part of his pants had been torn off below the knee and his lower leg had been wrapped in thick brown bandages that looked like some sort of animal skin.

"I wouldn't worry," Sage said. "I think they know how to treat him."

"They?" Sorren said. "Where are we? What happened?" All he knew was that he was sitting on a small cot on a small bed in a small wooden hut. Other than the bed, there was not much in the room. A torch, a few smoking incense sticks, and some small plants growing in wooden bowls. The place was clearly not meant to be lived in.

"We crashed into Owl's Fortress last night, several miles from here," Sage said. "I tried to treat you and Thale myself, but there wasn't much I could do. No supplies. A group of people showed up and brought you and Thale here where they could treat you. They call this place Owl's Grave. I've never heard of it. Have you?"

Sorren shook his head, slowly sliding his legs off the bed. "Where's my staff?"

"I hid it," Sage said. "Back on the airship. I wasn't sure if these people would help us if they knew who you really were. Well, *are.*"

"Who are these people?" Sorren asked.

"I haven't asked many questions," Sage said. "I told them we were merchants making deliveries to the Chosen One when our engine exploded. I think they believe it. Anyway, they told me to try waking you and inviting you to dinner. And I have something for you." Sage held up a stick, long and knotty, thinner than his staff.

"A stick," Sorren said, taking it.

"To walk with," Sage said.

"I would never have guessed. How's the airship?" Sorren asked, pulling himself up and leaning on the stick, careful to put no weight on his right leg.

"Damaged," Sage said. "Of course."

"Damaged," Sorren repeated quietly. He hobbled over to a window. Outside, the night sky was hidden by the thick branches of the forest's coniferous trees. No Nyrish moon. Not even a speck of its blue moonlight. Only thin strands of stars broke through the canopy.

Sorren imagined the world swirling into that black void in the sky. He could still feel it pulling at him, trying to suck him in, trying to swallow him whole. So that was how his father had been defeated. That was why Kovola hadn't been able find his body. He'd been sucked into the void.

Sorren wondered what it would be like to die in the void. Would you freeze to death? Would you suffocate, choking in agony on the nothingness? Would you disintegrate, your body torn apart by the vacuum? Would you simply cease to exist? How did the world work beyond that portal to the void?

Quove flew to Sorren's shoulder, closer to his neck than she usually landed.

"How badly is the airship damaged?" Sorren asked, pulling on his long black coat. "Can you repair it? How long will it take?"

Sage scoffed. "Does it matter?"

Sorren turned and looked at the man.

"You tried," Sage said. "And we almost died. You know you're no match for him."

Sorren was not about to just give up. He felt he was getting closer to something, like he was uncovering some secret. And now the Chosen One had once again seen him face to face. The Chosen One would know that one last Candlewood wizard lived. It was far too late for turning back.

Still, Sorren didn't feel like arguing. "We're going to have to repair the airship anyway," he said, flipping up the collar of his coat. "I don't intend to live here."

"The damage isn't bad," Sage said. "Just smashed up compressors and an overheated pressure chamber. Should only take a day to repair, but I don't have the tools."

"Do they have any tools here?" Sorren asked.

Sage shrugged. "I haven't asked many questions."

"I'm invited to dinner, you said?"

Sage nodded.

Sorren limped toward the door, grateful that his energy was returning, both to his body and his mind. He was looking forward to getting some food in his system. He couldn't remember the last time he'd had a decent meal. As he walked out of the hut and into the dark of the forest outside, he remembered the face of the woman with the dark colorful hair. Her voice echoed in his mind like something from a half-remembered dream. *Welcome to Owl's Grave.*

FIFTEEN

I T FELT STRANGE to hold such a thin short stick in his hand. He had already grown used to the cool lines of iron curling under his palm. Without his staff, he felt like he was incomplete. Still, there were plenty of spells he could cast without his staff. It was not as if he *needed* his staff.

Sorren followed a narrow trail between the trees and thick underbrush, the path lined with torches that lit the way. A rich scent of pine filled the air.

After walking for half a minute, a bluish-green light appeared in the distance, the flickering light of some large bonfire. Men were talking, children were laughing and shouting. People were playing lively tunes on mountain whistles and singing lighthearted songs that Sorren had never heard before.

Sorren approached the clearing. The bluish-green fire seemed like something from a witch's spell. There must've been forty or fifty people surrounding the fire, standing in huddled groups or sitting on wide logs like people in old paintings, casting long shadows on the trees behind them. Some had turtle shell bowls in their hands, eating some sort of soup or stew. They were dressed in wild assortments of animal skins, dark leathers and furs and feathers. Animal body parts like large paws, long tails, sharp teeth, and black eyes remained intact on some of their robes, as if the people were in fact half human and half beast.

The songs faded and a silence fell over them as Sorren stepped toward the bluish-green fire. They turned and stared at him. They were not vicious or accusing stares, as if he were a dangerous or unwelcome guest. They were eager stares, as if they'd been waiting for him and hoped he would say something.

But Sorren said nothing as he slowly limped closer the fire. He wasn't sure what to do with so much attention. He wasn't the son of a dark wizard to these people. He didn't know how to act.

A woman stepped toward him. Maewyn. Her name came to his mind without thinking. Her colorful hair almost seemed to glow in the firelight. She was just as tall as Sorren, and their eyes were level with each other.

"We're glad you were well enough to come," she said, smiling, holding out her arms and offering him assistance. Long wooden bracelets swung from her wrists. Sorren let her help him to a vacant space on a nearby log, where they sat next to each other. "Shadowvin, yes?"

"Shadowvin?" Sorren repeated.

"I told them your name," Sage said from behind. Sorren hadn't heard him following. "I didn't think you'd care."

"I'm still a bit tired," Sorren said.

"You have mirkglen powder flowing through your blood," Maewyn said. She was sitting too close. Sorren could almost feel her breath on his face. He wanted to lean away, but resisted. As if reading his thoughts, Maewyn shifted away, putting some space between them. "Is this your raven? She would not leave your side."

Quove still sat on his shoulder. The raven watched Maewyn cautiously and curiously. Perhaps the bird didn't like something about the strange brown fur hanging over Maewyn's shoulders.

Sorren put a silver-copper finger in front of the bird, Quove hopped onto it, and Sorren held her out in front. "She came to me when I was child."

A small boy, three or four years old and dressed in the black fur of some sort of mountain tiger, walked over to his side, glaring at his mechanical arm. Sorren considered smiling at the child, but wondered if that would only frighten him.

Sage sat on Sorren's left side and tapped the mechanical arm with his knuckles. "See?" he said. "I told you he had a silver arm."

The boy laughed, as if this were some sly joke.

Maewyn smiled at the child, then turned back to Sorren. "We were waiting for you to wake," Maewyn said. "What's your story?"

His story? Sorren could feel the eyes on him. He half expected someone to point and shout his real name, to reveal who he really was. Maybe part of him was hoping for it. He stared into the fire ahead, trying to dream up a new person he could be for the night.

"I grew up in the north," he said. "In Vonlock's castle, actually. My father was one of his guards. I was training to become one too, but . . . I lost my arm in an accident. My father was furious. I ran away by hiding on one of Sage's airships. As it turned out, he was looking for help on his ship and hired me."

"A runaway from Vonlock's castle," a man covered in wolf fur said with a hint of laughter. "Funny he should fall into Owl's Grave!"

The crowd chuckled.

"It *is* interesting that fate brought you here," Maewyn said. "They are all from the north too. They all worked for Vonlock at one time or another."

Sorren glanced around the fire, meeting the eyes of the faces staring at him, wondering if he'd recognize anyone. He didn't.

"It was years and years ago," the man in wolf fur said. The wolf's head hung down over his chest as if it were trying to bite through the man's skin and devour his heart. "We were sentenced to death." His smile had faded.

"It was the prophecy," Maewyn said. "The Candlewood Prophecy. The Wizard King was terrified of it. He began killing boys born in the eleventh month." Maewyn looked into the fire. "Every family here has lost a son at Vonlock's hand."

"Every boy in the kingdom born in the eleventh month?" Sorren asked. Why had he never heard of such a slaughter?

"Not the entire kingdom," Maewyn said. "The prophecy said the boy would be born under the king's own shadow. He only looked through the families that worked and lived in his castle."

"We were sentenced to death ourselves," the man in wolf fur said, "but we managed to escape. We fled south. Soldiers chased us, but by some miracle we survived."

"It was the prophecy," another man said, an old man with a short gray beard, dressed in dark bear skin, the bear's mighty paws sitting on his shoulders. "We had to survive so that the prophecy could be fulfilled."

The Chosen One's face seemed to appear in the bluish-green flames ahead, staring out at Sorren with a fire's eyes. Sorren glanced down at the forest floor, trying to forget the image.

"Yes," Maewyn said, "you are thinking the right thing. A pregnant woman fled with them. She gave birth on the eleventh day of the eleventh month. Atlorus was born and raised here, in my home, Owl's Grave."

"Atlorus is from Owl's Grave?" Sorren said.

Maewyn nodded. "You were just sleeping in his bed."

A young woman dressed in deer skin approached Sorren, a turtle shell bowl in her hands, the handle of a spoon pointing out over its edge. "Here," she said, holding out the bowl. "You should eat something."

Sorren let Quove hop back onto his shoulder, and he took the bowl with both hands. Steam rose from it and Sorren inhaled its warm exotic scent, a citrus perhaps, like some sort of strange fruit.

When he peered into the bowl, he almost dropped it. It seemed to be some sort of soup made of dead mangled caterpillars, seaweed, and mushrooms, all floating in a thick green syrup sprinkled with dirt and dead ants.

"Mmmm," Sage said, leaning toward the bowl. "I must say, that smells so goo— . . . Oh . . . Oh."

"Oh, yes, Bovadir is our best cook," Maewyn said. The young woman smiled and bowed. "This is a very difficult soup to make."

"I'm sure it is," Sage said.

The young woman turned to him. "I will fill a shell for you now."

"No, no, no!" Sage quickly waved a hand. "I'm full. I ate too much for lunch."

"Try it," Maewyn said, elbowing Sorren's arm. "It will help you heal."

Sorren grasped the spoon in his flesh-and-blood hand and swirled the concoction around, his stomach churning at the sight. He collected a hearty chunky spoonful and let it drip for a moment. He wanted these people to trust him. To *like* him, if possible. He wasn't Sorren tonight. He was Shadowvin here. He stuffed the spoon in his mouth.

Don't vomit, he told himself. *Do. Not. Vomit.* He began chewing. The syrup was thick and slippery, like an egg's yolk. Most of the chunky ingredients were soft and chewy, but every now and then something crunched and brushed against his tongue like sand. It all had a strange tangy taste, sweet and bitter at the same time.

Still, Sorren managed to keep from grimacing. He ate as if he were hungry and fascinated by the new tastes. He couldn't bring himself to smile, but he tried not to hesitate between spoonfuls.

As he ate quietly, the crowd seemed to lose interest in him, and they turned back to their songs and conversations. Children ran around behind the logs, playing tag or something like it. Now and then, Sorren could feel the children's eyes on him, watching him cautiously or staring at his arm. He almost wanted to cast some sort of spell to surprise them and make them laugh. He could probably lift one of the smaller ones a few feet into the air. But it would probably only terrify them. Besides, he didn't want to reveal that he was a wizard. Or the son of the Wizard King who destroyed their families and livelihoods, for that matter.

The man dressed in wolf skin approached with a wide wooden chalice. "Our finest tumbleberry juice," he said, offering the cup to Sorren.

Sorren took the cup and drank a sip. It was heavenly compared to the soup. He let it wash over his tongue.

"Do you have tools?" Sage asked.

"Tools?" the man said. "What sort of tools?"

"Building tools, fixing tools," Sage said. "I need to fix my airship."

"We can help you with that," the man said. "But not until next week. We need our tools for the hunt. We set a lot of traps."

"The hunt?" Sage asked.

"That's what we're celebrating tonight," the man said, waving a hand at the small crowd around the fire. "It's the night before our final hunt. Atlorus will be crowned king soon, and we intend to finally return north. Perhaps into the castle itself! We'll help you with your airship after the hunt."

Sage thanked him, and the man left. Then he turned to Sorren. "I guess we'll have to wait here for a week."

"You told us you were delivering something to Atlorus before your airship fell," Maewyn said. "Did you talk to him? Is he well?"

Sage said nothing. Sorren made no response as he finished chewing a mouthful of soup.

"We've been so afraid for him," Maewyn said. "I think, deep in our hearts, some of us doubted him. Some of us truly thought he'd be killed. We only found out he succeeded two days ago, when he flew the royal airship overhead."

Sorren finished chewing and swallowed. "Did *you* doubt him?" he asked.

Maewyn placed her hands together on her lap and looked forward into the fire. "It wasn't that I doubted him. It's the prophecy that troubles me. Prophecies are not always what they seem."

"Ah," Sage said. "You *are* Maewyn the Prophecy Keeper, aren't you? I thought it was you."

"Yes," Maewyn said. "That is, I was a prophecy keeper for a time."

"I know your work well," Sage said.

"Only a small portion of my work was ever published," Maewyn said. "Prophecies are like stories. You cannot write them down and be done with them. They are living things. They speak to those who can hear their secrets. They persuade people to take certain paths." She took in a deep breath. "I did not reveal all my research in my books. Some things are too dangerous to reveal. And some things cannot be revealed with words." She turned away from the fire. "But I knew Atlorus would not die at Vonlock's hand. Did you see him? Did you talk to him? I imagine he would be fascinated to see your silver arm."

"We saw him," Sorren said, scraping the bottom of bowl, thankful his stomach was not convulsing. "We didn't say anything. We only acknowledged each other." He swallowed his last spoonful and washed it down with the rest of the tumbleberry juice. "I am curious about something as well. Do you know *how* he killed the Wizard King?"

"Is that the question the kingdom is wondering?" Maewyn shivered and adjusted the furs hanging around her shoulder. "It is a secret, I'm afraid. I cannot speak of it."

Sorren let a few moments of silence pass. He didn't want to seem *too* curious. "Why is it a secret?"

"Some things are safer as secrets," Maewyn said matter-of-factly. She tilted her head. "What were you delivering, exactly?" She asked it tenderly, as though she knew it was a lie.

"Uh," Sage answered quickly, "it was, um . . . only some, uh . . . it was only . . . um . . . boxes of . . ."

"We were delivering a message," Sorren said.

"A message?" Maewyn said. "What message?"

Sorren pretended to hesitate. "I'd rather not say. As you said, some things are safer as secrets."

Maewyn stared at him, not saying a word. Sorren held her gaze, studying the shades of her blue moonlight eyes. When she spoke, she spoke in a quiet voice, as if her words were for Sorren only. "I think I know what sort of message you had. These people think they'll leave the forest soon. But I don't think it'll be soon." A warm slow breeze ruffled her hair. "There is still a darkness that must pass. A shadow drifts over the kingdom. I think you can feel it too, can't you? I can see it in your eyes." Somehow, her stare grew deeper, as if she were looking into his mind. "I think you are like me. I think you know things no one else can see." Her head turned slightly toward the flames, her skin glowing purple in the burning light. Her voice was a slow and careful whisper now. "Are you here because your airship crashed? Or are you hiding?" She glanced up into the night sky. "Be careful while you're here. The owls know who you are."

They sat in silence for some time, watching the fire.

The night grew quiet. The chattering stopped. The children tired of running and shouting. Everyone seemed to grow still. Only one whistle played on. A woman sitting by herself on the other side of the fire, her eyes seemingly lost in a spell as she played a low melody on a long mammoth bone whistle, her fingers gentle and graceful. The tune was slow and melancholy. For a moment, it turned Sorren back into a small child in a warm castle. He had been ill one stormy night, and his father kept him close to the fire, wrapped in blankets, and told him stories. He had looked out through a window and had been frightened by the lightning, but his father had told him he had more power flowing through his blood than the winds of a winter storm. Then he had pointed to the kingdom below, stretching far into the distance, and reminded him that someday he'd be the king, and more powerful than the rage of a thousand storms.

When the song ended, the only sound was the flames of

the bluish-green fire licking the empty air. Some sat still, lost in their thoughts. Children had fallen asleep in their parents' arms. Slowly, they began to rise, stretching, collecting their empty bowls and cups. Everyone spoke in hushed voices, as if there were something still floating in the air that had to remain undisturbed.

"A lullaby for her son," Maewyn said quietly. "Atovin plays it every night."

"What happened to her son?"

Maewyn did not answer immediately. She let the question linger in the air like the end of the song. Then she answered slowly, "He was taken from her, for a time. He was born to endure darkness, to suffer trials, to see death." She took a slow breath. "Perhaps you feel it too, in the coolness of the winds. That the prophecy is not yet fulfilled. That his journey is not yet over."

Sorren stared at the woman on the other side of the fire, and realized he had already known. "Her son is Atlorus."

"Her son is Atlorus."

SIXTEEN

LATER THAT NIGHT, Sorren followed Sage along the winding forest pathways to the small hut Thale had been placed in. The pine trees overhead rustled in the wind and owls hooted from somewhere in the shadows above. Sage pointed ahead. "It's that one there. Don't wake him." Sage had made a small fuss about leading Sorren to Thale's hut when he'd asked, complaining that Maewyn and the healers of Owl's Grave did not want the boy disturbed while he was healing. But it was Sorren's fault he and Thale were injured and stranded in this forest. He had to at least see the boy.

Sorren began limping toward the small hut, but paused before entering. "We should be able to fix the airship tomorrow evening. You'll have to decide whether you want to leave with me or stay here with Thale."

"What?" Sage said. "We won't have the tools for a week. And *I* will fix the airship, not you. You rely too much on your spells. Makes for lazy, sloppy work."

"We'll have the tools tomorrow," Sorren said. He wasn't about to spend a week in Owl's Grave.

"But they said the hunt will last—"

"I will get the tools," Sorren said.

"You're just going to steal them?" Sage asked. "I don't even know where they keep them."

"Don't worry about it. Go get some sleep."

"Be careful," Sage said. "I have a feeling you don't want to anger these people."

"They can't hurt me," Sorren said.

"I just don't want them angry with *me*," Sage said as he turned and began to leave. "I don't want to have to depend on *you* for protection."

"But you do," Sorren said.

Sage put his arms out, waving at the forest surrounding them. "And look where it brought me." Then he disappeared between the trees.

Sorren pushed open the door to Thale's hut. It was dim inside. The only light came from a small lantern with a bluish-green flame inside, the same sort of color the bonfire had been. Thale lay on a bed against the back wall, wrapped in thick gray and white furs. His tovocular eye sat on the top of a barrel beside the bed—his empty eye socket was a dark shadow. His face was covered in cuts and scratches, most likely from the airship's shattered windows, but none looked very deep. Sorren could hardly judge the severity of his other injuries with so many blankets piled over him, but he wasn't about to disturb them.

Sorren knew he'd have to leave Thale in Owl's Grave for

some time to heal. This was probably the safest place for him. There were no mirrors in Owl's Grave for Sorren to enchant, so it would be some time before he'd be able to use a portal to get Thale back to the caverns.

"Sorren?" Thale asked, his real eye squinting open.

"You're supposed to be sleeping."

"Thought I heard voices. Can you hand me my eye?" He pulled an arm out from under the blankets and held out his hand.

Sorren handed him his tovocular eye. "How do you feel?"

"Fine," Thale said, "only tired."

"They have strong medicines."

"Kovola will be so angry with me," Thale said, pushing his eye into his socket. It began whirling around, pointed at Sorren. "I'm a terrible student."

"Kovola won't be angry with you," Sorren said, studying the rest of the room. Like Sorren's hut, it was mostly empty, only some small plants, some incense, and some lanterns.

"He said to me . . ." Thale said. "He warned me not to, he told me not to . . . Well . . ."

"He'll be angry with *me*," Sorren said, flicking some lanterns on and off with the Nyrish power. "I brought you here. He can hardly blame you for this. I'm selfish, arrogant, reckless . . ."

"I can't understand any of the readings he assigns," Thale said. "It's all like a foreign language anymore."

"His oath to my family is the only reason he stays with me," Sorren said. "He'd be dead if he broke it—the Nyrish power has him bound. Don't worry about Kovola."

"It's only that . . . I don't . . ." Thale's mouth made shapes, but it seemed he couldn't find the words. After a moment, he gave up, and lay there listless. Then he took a deep breath. "I don't think I really care about tove making. Not anymore."

Sorren made no reply.

"But," Thale shook his head, "I can't do anything else! And Kovola *wants* to teach me. And he saved my life and he made me my eye." He pulled out his tovocular eye and turned it around in his hand. "I think I owe him."

Sorren flicked all the lanterns off, save for the one that had been lit when he entered. "We can solve this later. Don't let it worry you. For now, rest."

Thale sighed, placing his golden tovocular eye back on top of the barrel. "I'm having strange dreams with these medicines." He closed his eye and pulled his arm back under the blankets. "Or maybe it's being in a bed that isn't mine."

"If you never leave home, you'll never be homesick," Sorren said. He clutched his walking stick and limped out of the hut, carefully closing the door behind him.

There were more owls hooting in the shadows now. Sorren couldn't see any of them, but he knew they were there, watching.

SEVENTEEN

A T DAWN, SAGE lightly knocked on the door to Sorren's hut. "Sorren?" He slowly pushed the door open. "Awake yet, Sorren?"

But the hut was empty. The lanterns and sticks of incense had been extinguished. Sorren's walking stick was propped up against the bed, which looked as if it hadn't been used the night before, its blankets folded neatly on top. Not even the young wizard's raven was sitting around. Sage took the walking stick with him and left the hut.

The men, women, and children of Owl's Grave were gathered in a wide clearing not far from where the bonfire had been roaring the night before. They stood in small groups or sat on long pine logs scattered throughout the clearing, hunched over wooden bowls and plates, eating breakfast. Cloaked in their wild furs, they all looked like strange beasts from ancient legends.

Sage scanned the small crowd until he spotted Maewyn.

Her blue and purple hair made her stand out. She sat next to a small group of children, enthusiastically talking with them about something. Sage approached her from behind. She turned as he neared, as if she'd been expecting him. The children glanced up at him.

"We have bread, porridge, sausage," Maewyn said, pointing to the side of the clearing where trays of food sat on several tables. A wide steaming pot hung over a small fire, where a young man stood ladling out something thick and creamy to people holding out their bowls. "Help yourself," Maewyn said, smiling.

Sage held out Sorren's walking stick. "Have you seen So . . . um . . . Shadowvin? He left his walking stick by his bed."

"He left," Maewyn said.

"Left?"

"He went with the hunt," a boy sitting beside Maewyn said. He looked to be around nine or ten years old, and wore a hat that looked like it had once been a raccoon. Its tail hung down the side of his face. "My brother's on the hunt too."

"The hunt?" Sage repeated.

"The final hunt of the season," Maewyn said. "It's what we were preparing for last night. Your friend Shadowvin insisted on joining the hunting team."

"He said he was a great hunter," the boy with the raccoon hat said.

"Is he not?" Maewyn asked.

"It's not something he ever bragged to me about," Sage said. He twisted the walking stick in his hand. "So his leg is healed already?"

"It's unlikely," Maewyn said. "But he didn't seem to be in any pain."

Sage leaned on the walking stick, wondering how much pain Sorren was forcing himself through. "The hunt lasts a week, right?"

"Usually," Maewyn said. "It depends on how much they catch, and how quickly. Why? Will Shadowvin slow the team down? Did we make a mistake letting him go? He *is* quite young."

"Even younger than my brother," the raccoon-hat boy said.

Sage finally understood what Sorren was doing. He was going to use his wizardry to help with the hunt and speed things along. Then they'd get the tools they needed to repair the airship. Sage only hoped Sorren wouldn't reveal his identity in the process. If any of these people discovered he was a wizard of the Nyrish power . . .

"Is something wrong?" Maewyn asked.

Sage realized he was staring off into the forest with a blank expression. He faked a smile and looked at Maewyn and the children. "No," he said. "Shadowvin will be fine. He'll do well on the hunt." He jabbed the walking stick in the air, mimicking a spear being driven into a wild animal. "He enjoys that sort of thing." He dug the bottom of the walking stick into the dirt and left it sticking out of the ground like some sad branchless tree. "I, on the other hand, enjoy a hot meal." And he walked off for some breakfast.

$\star$ $\star$ $\star$ $\star$ $\star$

"**A**ND WHAT'S the largest animal one could catch?" Sorren asked as he followed the hunting team, trudging through the forest's thick underbrush. Every step sent icy pain shooting up through his leg, but he ignored it.

The leader of the hunting team, Rozzom, looked back over his shoulder. "That would be a rire," he said. He wore the same wolf skin he'd worn the night before, only now the wolf's head sat atop his own like a hat, giving him the appearance that his face was being swallowed whole under the dead creature's long fangs.

There were thirteen members of the hunting team. Most were older than thirty and they carried spears and knives, crossbows and swords. Three were in their late teens or early twenties. Sorren had made himself the fourteenth and youngest member. For now, he walked behind the rest of the team, keeping in stride with the second youngest member, a young man called Baylet. He was clad in the white furs of what looked like some strange giant mountain goat. A pair of sharp horns spiraled out of the fur on Baylet's head.

"A rire?" Sorren repeated. He had heard of the beasts, but had never actually seen one. He hadn't realized there were rires in these woods.

"Twice the size of a mountain bear," Baylet said. "They look like giant dogs. Long white fur with large patches of color."

I know what they look like, Sorren wanted to say. *I'm not a complete dolt.* But he held his tongue.

"We only ever caught one before," Baylet said. "Well, Rozzom did."

"With plenty of help," Rozzom said, leading the team up a steep incline. "Watch your step here." He grabbed hold of the dark mossy boulders protruding from the hill to pull himself up. "It takes at least three men to take down a rire. Don't go after one on your own. They can be very aggressive. I doubt it would even be worth our time trying to catch one, but if you see one, fourth whistle. Oh, wait." He paused halfway up the hill and turned back to face Sorren. "You don't have a whistle, Shadowvin, do you?"

"No," Sorren said.

"I completely forgot to bring extras," Rozzom said.

"I have an extra," Baylet said, padding the tools and equipment dangling from his belt. "Here," he said, holding out a narrow whistle, two hand-widths in length. "Used to be my father's."

Sorren took the whistle. It seemed like a delicate piece of artwork. Intricate designs were carved along its sides, tiny images of men running through forests, swimming across rivers, and staring up at the moons. They almost seemed to tell a story.

As the team continued deeper into the forests, Baylet taught Sorren how they used the whistles to send different signals through the forest. "First whistle" meant game had been spotted and to be quiet and alert until further notice. "Second whistle" meant the game had escaped. "Third whistle" meant game had been caught. "Fourth whistle" meant game had been spotted and assistance was needed. "Fifth whistle" meant it was time to gather for a break. Finally, "sixth whistle" was a distress signal, a call for help.

Sorren practiced each signal as quietly as he could until he was confident he remembered all of them.

"Oh, and we're not allowed to kill any owls," Baylet said.

"Why not?" Sorren asked.

Baylet shrugged. "Bad luck I guess. Maewyn says that they protect us. That this is their forest."

"I haven't even seen any owls yet," Sorren said.

"They do keep their distance." Baylet glared up at the branches above. "But they're somewhere up there. A whole army of them."

Sorren thought about warning the team not to kill any ravens either. He didn't want Quove getting an arrow through the heart. But he knew it wouldn't be necessary. Quove could take care of herself.

The hunting team walked more slowly now. Sorren guessed by the light of the sky that it was two or three hours until noon. It was odd being awake during daylight. It felt as if the world belonged to different people. Sorren almost felt abandoned without the Nyrish moon in the sky to draw power from. Not that he needed to draw power from it every day. But it was comforting to know it was up there among the stars.

An older man called Entackus approached Sorren. He sported a short gray beard and was dressed in bear skin. "You know how to work a crossbow, yes?" he asked, holding out a well-used model of the weapon. Earlier that morning, Sorren had insisted that he was a very experienced hunter, claiming he'd been trained in the skill while training to be guard.

Throwing knives at a tree had convinced the leaders that his skills would be useful.

Sorren didn't take the crossbow, but instead held out his silver-copper arm. "A spear."

Entackus raised his eyebrows. In a growly voice, he called out to a man in the distance. "Do you have an extra spear?"

A moment later, a spear came soaring through the air, its razor-sharp tip pointing straight at the short bearded man. He stepped to the side and caught it firmly in his right hand as if it were child's play. He whirled the spear upright so that its tip pointed skyward and held it out toward Sorren. "A spear," he said.

Sorren took it and tested its weight in his grip. It was thin but sturdy, heavy, and almost twice his height. The sharp stone arrow that formed its tip looked as if it had been carved with as much care as the bone whistle, though it lacked any ornamentation. Two long black and brown owl feathers were tied just underneath the arrow, where the stone met the wood. Sorren flung the spear upward, changing his grip on it, and pointed it at an imaginary beast before him.

"Can you handle it?" the bearded man asked.

"It'll work," Sorren said, setting the spear by his side, leaning on it a bit to relieve some of the pain in his leg.

The bearded man took a step back and looked Sorren up and down as if he wasn't sure what to make of him. "Good luck."

Sorren nodded in return and the two continued following the rest of the team through the brush.

★   ★   ★   ★   ★

A HALF-HOUR LATER, Rozzom instructed the hunters to split into pairs and pointed them in the directions they were to explore. Some of the older men carried bags of tools, strands of ropes, bundles of nets, rolls of blankets, and some sort of beast hide. Rather than hunting, they would no doubt be setting traps and pitching camp. After all, they were expecting the hunt to last a week. Sorren intended to end it much sooner than that.

Sorren was not surprised to be paired with Baylet. Apparently Rozzom thought Sorren would make a great tutor for Baylet. Sorren didn't want a student, much less a hunting partner, but he had to go along with Rozzom's commands, at least for now. It wouldn't do any good to argue here.

Sorren let Baylet lead the way, and they walked what seemed like a mile from the other hunters before stopping to rest. Baylet spread a thin length of bear skin under a half-dead pine tree, covering the layer of dead needles that blanketed the ground. Sorren propped his spear up against the tree and slowly sat, adjusting his long dark coat to cover his leg, where bandages still hid his wound.

As Baylet sat beside Sorren, he kept a crossbow clutched in his hands as if it were as precious as a newborn infant.

"You've fired it before, haven't you?" Sorren asked.

Baylet gently put the crossbow at his side and dug into a small satchel under his goat-skin coat. "Are you hungry?" he asked.

"What do you have?" Sorren said.

"Bread, fruit, nuts. Just snacks." He pulled out a pair of thin copper flasks and tossed one to Sorren. "Water. If you're thirsty."

Sorren twisted the cap off and took a few sips.

"Apple?" Baylet asked.

Sorren held out a hand and took it. It had been a long time since he'd had an apple. He didn't like them. Too crunchy. But he wasn't Sorren right now. He was Shadowvin. If Shadowvin could down that disgusting stew last night without making faces and vomiting, he could accept an apple. He casually bit into it.

Swallowing, Sorren pointed at the crossbow. "You've used it before?" he asked again.

Baylet nodded and swallowed a mouthful of bread. He opened his mouth, but didn't say anything.

Sorren noticed Quove not far away, sitting on a thin branch in the tree ahead of them, pecking at insects.

"I'm good with a crossbow," Baylet finally said. "There's a secret to it."

"A secret?"

"To hunting in general." Baylet held up a hand and wriggled his fingers. "You have to master aiming, triggering. Holding your weapon. The physical side of it. But there's more to it." He took another bite of his biscuit and tapped his forehead. "You have think the right thing," he said, his mouth half full.

"You have to focus," Sorren said.

Baylet shook his head, swallowing. "No. I mean . . . yes, but there's more. You have to . . ." Baylet grew silent and still, his eyes fixed on the crossbow at his side, between him and Sorren. Then he put his half eaten biscuit down and put his fingers to his chest. "It might sound silly but . . . You have to fill your heart with something."

Sorren made no response. He took another bite of his apple and watched Quove on her branch. She had her head stretched backward, preening the feathers on her back.

"Do you know what I fill my heart with?" Baylet said. "Do you know what puts me in the right mindset?"

Sorren turned to face him.

"The Wizard King who killed my brother." Baylet's eyes seemed to darken as he said it. "Vonlock. I see him in the teeth of the all the creatures I kill. It helps me aim, helps me pull the trigger. And then I can hunt. And then I *want* to hunt. Because if it weren't for him, I'd know my brother." The young man put a hand on the crossbow. "So I think about the dark wizard and the brother I never met. And then I don't miss. That's what I mean by filling your heart with something." He looked up at Sorren. "Do you have something like that? Something you can fill your heart with? Something you can see in the animals?"

Sorren rolled the apple from his flesh-and-blood hand into his mechanical hand and held it tightly, almost crushing it. He slowly turned his hand this way and that, examining how his silver fingers clutched the fruit.

"Shadowvin?" Baylet asked.

Sorren didn't answer.

"Oh," Baylet said, shivering, pulling at the fur that hung over his shoulders. "Cold winds in these parts. The owls know something."

Sorren took another bite of the apple, wiping the juice that dripped down his chin. "The owls know something?"

"It's what Maewyn says whenever she gets a chill," Baylet said. "That the owls know something. That the owls are warning her."

Sorren studied the branches above. Thin branches, thin green needles, slivers of a cloudy blue sky. No owls in sight. *You people and your owls may drive me mad before I escape your forest*, he thought.

Sorren stretched out his flesh-and-blood hand, resting it on Baylet's shoulder. "I do fill my heart with something," he said. Then he slowly inhaled, pulling Baylet's energy out of him and collecting it into himself. Baylet's head dropped forward and his eyes fluttered and closed before he fell sideways, fast asleep.

"Get some rest," Sorren said, tossing his half eaten apple out into the forest and grabbing his spear. He turned to Quove and whistled. The raven flew ahead and Sorren followed.

EIGHTEEN

"**Y**OU'LL KNOW it's him by his mechanical arm," Atlorus said to the group of four soldiers standing before the edge of Owl's Fortress. "Don't let him see you. And don't hurt anyone but him. Owl's Grave is my home. If you never see him alone, then don't attack."

Atlorus wasn't even sure Sorren had survived the crash in his tiny cargo ship, but it was impossible to land the royal airship in the thick forest to find out. Sending in a small group of soldiers with a number of hand bombs was all he could think to do without venturing into the forest himself. He did not have time for such an adventure. Now that he'd seen Sorren alive with his own eyes, he wanted to be crowned king as soon as possible. Then he'd be able to form an army of his own and wouldn't have to depend on Gashdane and his foreign Zolen soldiers.

"You have your orders, men," Gashdane said.

Atlorus spun around. He hadn't realized Gashdane was

behind him, watching. Gashdane stood there against the side of the airship, the hint of a smile on his lips.

"What is it?" Atlorus asked as the Zolen soldiers began disappearing into the forest.

"You've changed," Gashdane said. "Gone is the nervous frightened boy who never wanted to leave his home."

In his fist, Atlorus rolled the black crystal against his palm. "I almost had him."

"You'll have him in the end," Gashdane said. "It's the prophecy. His death is written in the stars."

Atlorus walked up the bay door bridge, back aboard the grand airship. "Let's return to the castle now."

"But you still have more—"

"I want to be crowned," Atlorus said. "If I ever see Sorren again, I want him to see the Chosen One on his throne. Then I'll finish him."

NINETEEN

EVEN THOUGH he walked alone, and even though every step sent the pain of a twisting knife shooting up his leg, Sorren refused to let himself limp. He followed the shadow of his raven through the trees, trusting the bird to lead him to game. Quove was the real hunter here, after all. She often survived on catching and eating mice and baby squirrels.

Sorren clutched the spear in his mechanical hand, using it like a walking stick, poking it into the ground with each step. With his flesh-and-blood hand, he reached out to run his fingers along the bark of the passing trees and through the branches that twisted out toward him, letting the needles stab his skin and make his fingers sticky.

After some ten minutes of venturing further through the forest, Sorren's raven began to slow. She'd linger on a branch, then fly to another, pausing before flying again. Sorren knew they must be getting close to whatever creature the bird was leading him to.

Finally, Quove flew to a branch and kept there, turning back to face Sorren. Sorren watched her for a moment to be sure she didn't intend to fly off again, then began scanning his surroundings. Surely something was near.

Thud.

A sound in the distance, like a giant stone slamming into the ground.

Thud.

Sorren held his spear close. The forest ahead was an endless labyrinth of trees. Small puddles of what little sunlight broke through the canopy freckled the forest floor, shimmering in and out of each other, dancing to the soundless rhythms of the wind.

Thud.

The slow but steady footsteps of a beast. Sorren saw something move between the trees in the distance, a fleck of white.

Thud.

It was slowly coming his way. Sorren had to hide. That way, he could take the creature by surprise. He turned to the branches above and whispered a spell to them. Slowly, they bent down like a mother's arms, curling around him and pulling him from the ground. He whispered a few more spells to them, arranging them around so that he had a clear view of the forest below. It was hardly comfortable being wrapped in the branches of a pine tree with all its needles, but Sorren was more focused on staying as quiet as possible.

The slow footsteps continued.

Thud.

Thud.

Thud.

Closer and closer.

Sorren readied the spear in his silver-copper hand, turning it so that the stone arrow at its end pointed downward. Now there was nothing but to watch and wait.

Thud.

Thud.

Thud.

Finally, the beast came into view. It was a rire. Just as Sorren had hoped. It looked larger than the ones he'd seen in paintings. Three times the size of a mountain bear, with long scraggly strands of thick white fur, splotches of color splattered about like spilled paint, green here, blue there, red, purple, yellow. With its wide black triangular nose and large floppy ears, its head looked like a giant scruffy dog. It would look almost friendly if it weren't for the two long fangs that pointed down from under its top lip like a pair of white swords. Its eyes were large and night-sky black. Its head turned from side to side gently, as if it were curious, pondering everything in sight. With every step, it kept its shoulders and head held high, like a knight approaching his king.

It was the most majestic animal Sorren had ever seen.

Sorren aimed his spear at the rire, just below its head, at the side of its neck. *I'm sorry about this, my friend,* he thought.

But rather than utter the spell that would send the spear shooting through the forest air, Sorren hesitated and watched.

The rire was sniffing at the air, taking deep breaths as if it had caught some curious aroma. It began stepping in circles, every step both mighty and gentle. It moved like music, and Sorren was caught up in its soundless song. No painting could capture the grace of its dance. For a moment, Sorren forgot why he was there.

Something gray fluttered in the tree beside Sorren. Turning his gaze from the rire, he saw a large owl perched on a branch by his side, gray and black stripes running along its feathers, rings of gray framing its pale yellow eyes. Sorren met its wide-eyed stare. Craning its head, the owl looked at Sorren's mechanical hand and up and down the spear it held, as if wondering what the wizard might be doing.

Thud.

The owl turned and looked down at the rire below.

Sorren whispered a spell to the branches and they slowly lowered him to the forest floor. The rire was facing away from him, and he was careful to keep his movements as silent as possible, but dead twigs snapped beneath his feet and the rire froze.

Sorren stood up straight, once again pointing the spear at the mountain of white fur. The rire was at least twice his height. He could easily imagine the creature killing him with one swipe of its massive paw.

The rire began turning back around, and looked Sorren straight in the eye. It didn't seemed threatened or angered, even as Sorren pointed the spear at its neck. It continued sniffing at the air, watching Sorren.

Sorren almost wanted to pet the rire, to know how that thick white blanket of fur might feel beneath his hand. He'd know soon enough. He passed the spear from his mechanical hand to his flesh-and-blood hand. Without blinking, keeping his gaze upon the giant beast, he uttered a short spell to the breeze.

Instantly, a blast of wind took the spear from Sorren's hand, sent it racing through the air, and lodged it deep into the neck of the beast.

The rire groaned, or tried to, its cry coming out as a low gurgle. Its head turned skyward and it fell to its side, the ground rumbling as its body crashed against the forest floor. Above, dozens of owls flew from their hidden places in the trees, taking to the sky and vanishing. The rire kicked its legs, but they soon grew still. One last long breath escaped the rire's mouth and Sorren knew it was dead.

Quove flew to Sorren's shoulder as the wizard approached the fallen animal and put his flesh-and-blood hand on the creature's chest. The fur was soft and deep and warm, and Sorren let it run through his fingers. Then he found the bone whistle in his pocket and blew the signal.

Third whistle. Game had been caught.

"ARIRE!" Entackus said. "Look at this! A mother rire!" The hunters were racing forward, gathering around the dead beast with bright eyes and wide smiles. Some of them paced around the creature as if to inspect it, running their fingers through the animal's thick fur as Sorren had done.

"Very impressive, Shadowvin" Rozzom said, putting a hand on Sorren's shoulder. Sorren resisted the impulse to twist away from the man's grip. "You *are* a hunter, then, aren't you?"

"How did you bury this so deep?" Entackus asked, pulling at the spear projecting from rire's neck. "Rire skin isn't thin."

Sorren held up his silver-and-copper arm, curling his fingers. "I have an advantage."

Rozzom looked around. "Where's Baylet?"

"He fell asleep."

"Asleep? How could he fall asleep? He loves the hunt."

Sorren shrugged.

"So . . . you killed this by yourself?" Entackus asked, running a hand along one of the rire's long fangs.

"I did," Sorren said.

Entackus glanced at Rozzom. Just a quick glance with no expression, but Sorren knew it meant something between the two.

"I know how you did it," one of hunters smiled. He was clad in the furs of a pale yellow mountain cat. He walked toward the face of the rire, pointing at its eyes. "You weren't afraid. You looked her right in the eye and stood your ground. Gave her no reason to panic. Isn't that so?"

Rozzom clapped his hands. "Parthus and Tidas, go pack up the tents and the equipment. The hunt is over. Fendor, get the bags. We'll have to make multiple trips for all this meat. Let's start skinning her. Coridin, a sword."

One of the hunters tossed Rozzom a sword. It was a plain looking thing, with a bland hilt of dark rough leather and an undecorated scabbard. Rozzom unsheathed it and held it out to Sorren. "Would you like the honor?"

Sorren glanced at his half-reflection in the silver blade.

"What honor?"

Rozzom laughed. "Draining her."

"I'm not so practiced with that," Sorren said.

Rozzom laughed again and walked toward the rire's neck, motioning the other hunters to step back. He tugged at the spear protruding from the animal's neck, slowly slid it out, and tossed it aside. Then he raised the sword high above his head, adjusted his grip on the hilt, took a deep breath, and pulled it down in a swift slanted arc. The skin of the rire's neck ripped open and a torrent of dark red blood splashed out, oozing across the forest floor like a sudden flood, steam rising from its surface.

The hunters cheered.

Sorren looked away and leaned on a nearby tree, suddenly weak.

TWENTY

I T TOOK SEVERAL HOURS to walk home. But even the hunters carrying the largest loads of rire meat and sweating like melting snowmen seemed to march on in good spir-its, somehow finding the vim to raise their voices in song as the team trudged on. Sorren didn't recognize the melodies or lyrics of their ballads. They sounded like strange poems from ancient lands, songs about eagles and rivers and mountains and rising suns.

Sorren himself held a leather bag over his shoulder, clutching it in his mechanical hand, a load of muscle and meat that had been pulled from the rire's legs and massive paws. The smell was foul, but Sorren kept a small piece of pine branch in his other hand, holding it to his nose when he needed relief.

Baylet walked close by, carrying a wide basket of rire fur that the forest dwellers would no doubt use to make clothes. Baylet had been confused as to how he'd fallen asleep, but he seemed to remember little of his conversation with Sorren and wasn't asking questions. Perhaps he was embarrassed.

The sun was setting when they finally made it home, and the rest of Owl's Grave celebrated their early return with the fervor of a long awaited holiday. The children seemed fascinated by the rire fangs Rozzom had pulled from the animal's mouth and the strange colors of the animal's fur. The adults were quick to set up another bonfire, this time with flames of purple, blue, green, and orange. They began smearing pieces of meat with wild spices and slapping them on black pans.

Sorren handed over the bag he'd carried, receiving wide-eyed grins when Rozzom told the others that he was the one who'd slain the rire. They slapped his back and offered him drinks he didn't want but drank anyway.

As the sky grew black, a crowd formed around the bonfire, and drummers and whistlers began making their little songs. Sorren found Sage in the crowd, carrying around the walking stick Sorren had left behind.

Sorren was careful to keep his voice low. "The tools are ready, over there." He pointed to where the hunters had piled their traps and equipment. "We'll leave as soon as the ship is ready."

"Look at everyone," Sage said, waving the stick at the crowd. "They're all so excited. Don't you want to celebrate?"

Sorren ignored the question. "Have you decided whether or not to stay with Thale?"

Before Sage could respond, Thale stepped forward beside him. "I have to stay?" The boy leaned on a tall walking stick of his own, crouched to the side like an old man. Dark leather bandages covered one arm, which hung from his neck in a sling made of thin straps. His hair was a wild mess; he'd obviously rolled out of bed only recently. His blue and gold eye whirred, zooming out toward Sorren.

"You need more time to heal," Sorren said.

"I can heal in the caverns," Thale said. He leaned forward and whispered. "These people are mad. Their beds are uncomfortable, their food makes me gag, and I think they pray to the owls."

"They don't pray to the owls," Sage said, adjusting his spectacles. "They just admire them."

"And they . . . well . . . they smell," Thale said. "This whole place smells. I can't stay here."

"You should be in bed even now," Sage said.

"Come on, Sorren," Thale said.

"Shadowvin," Sage whispered.

Thale leaned forward, his movements slow and stiff. "Let's all leave this place together."

"You know what I'm after," Sorren said. "You saw what I'm up against. You're safer here."

Thale's shoulders slumped. He opened his mouth, paused, then closed it again.

"Shadowvin," someone said, tapping Sorren's shoulder. Sorren turned to see Rozzom, the wolf head he wore once again hanging across his chest. The man motioned for Sorren to follow him.

Sorren grabbed the walking stick from Sage. "My leg still hurts." He leaned on the stick as he limped along behind Rozzom, following him to a wide log that sat near the fire. Rozzom motioned for him to sit. A small crowd had gathered around the empty spot.

"What is it?" Sorren asked.

"Sit, sit, sit," Rozzom said.

Sorren sat.

Rozzom accepted a wide wooden platter from someone beside him. On top, something was wrapped in cloth. It was the size of a loaf of bread, but oddly shaped, like a stone found on a mountainside. Rozzom knelt down and held out the platter.

"As slayer of the rire, this is yours, Shadowvin," Rozzom said. "It's a tradition."

Sorren put his walking stick across his lap and took the bundle, pretending to be interested in the strange gift. It weighed about the same as a stone, but was soft and warm to the touch. He slowly unraveled the greasy cloth around it, already knowing what he'd find.

The chunk of meat sat there in his palms, well-cooked and steaming.

"The heart of the rire," Rozzom said, smiling, the side of his face outlined by the fire that roared behind him. "Have a bite."

What a horrible tradition, Sorren thought. He drew in a deep breath, closed his eyes, and pretended to be intoxicated by the scent of the offering. Then he brought the heart to his mouth and bit into it. The meat was chewy, and Sorren was pleased to find that it tasted more like burnt wood and strange spices than anything else.

When he finally swallowed, the small crowd around him rewarded his fake smile with light applause. A woman offered him a cup of some sort of juice, then they turned back to their own plates and drinks and conversations.

"I wish I could've seen you do it, Shadowvin," Rozzom said, placing the platter against the log beside Sorren and rising to his feet. "Is there any chance you'd be willing to teach us what you know?"

Sorren licked his teeth, trying to work out the bits of meat that had burrowed between them. "I'm afraid I may be gone tomorrow. Time is precious in our business."

"Ah, of course," Rozzom said. "We ourselves won't be here for very much longer. Just until we get word of Atlorus's coronation. Then it's back to the north, back to the castle. Perhaps we'll see you there someday."

Sorren nodded. "I'm sure of it."

Rozzom smiled politely and left.

Sorren stared at the fire before him, letting its heat warm his face, watching the colorful flames as they shifted and warped and curled into and out of each other like some endlessly flowing braid.

Sage walked up beside Sorren, whispering. "I'll work on the airship as soon as I get a bite to eat, all right? I'm starving."

"Here." Sorren wrapped the rire heart back in its cloth and shoved it into Sage's hands. "Take it with you."

"Oh, Sorren," Sage whispered, "must you be so heartless?"

"If you're not going to fix the ship, I will."

Sage grunted and held out a hand. "Give me your drink too."

Sorren took one last sip from his cup and handed it to Sage.

"Enjoy your celebration," Sage said. "I'll be back when I've finished."

"Don't bother," Sorren said. "I'll be there at midnight."

"How will you know when it's midnight?"

"The Nyrish moon."

Sage looked up. "Can you see it from here?"

"I don't have to *see* it," Sorren said.

Sage was silent for a moment, then whispered excitedly. "The Nyrish power! Of course! See, that's the sort of thing I need for my research. It means the energy from the Nyrish moon can be measured with a period equal to that of the rotation of the planet, which means if I can calculate—"

Sorren held up his silver-copper hand. "Put it in a book."

Sage grunted again and turned away, mumbling something to himself as he disappeared into the shadows of the night. Sorren thought he heard some rather impolite words in the air.

B EYOND THE BONFIRE'S clearing, invisible in the blackness of the forest's shadows, four Zolen soldiers stood behind trees, eyes peering through the branches.

"See that silver arm?" one of the Zolen soldiers whispered to his three comrades. "That's him. Sorren." He put a hand in the satchel that hung at his side.

Another soldier caught his arm. "Not yet. We have to wait until—"

"Until he's alone? Look at that crowd. He won't be alone tonight."

"Atlorus said not to hurt anyone else."

"Of course he did, he grew up here. But we have a chance to end this."

The other soldiers were silent.

"Here." The Zolen soldier began taking the small hand bombs from the satchel, handing them to his comrades. "We'll attack on my count. Five . . . Four . . . Three—"

"No," another soldier said. "We cannot hurry into this."

"If Sorren lives, the blood of his future victims will be on *our* hands. We *must* do this."

"Let's at least wait a bit. Perhaps the crowd will thin."

The Zolen soldier sighed, gripping a hand bomb. "I will *not* wait until it's too late."

"We won't. We'll only wait for the best moment to strike."

"Very well. Sorren dies tonight."

S ORREN WALKED to the other side of the colorful bonfire, where baskets of bread, bowls of fruits, cups of rice, and a large dish of steaming rire meat had been set out on narrow tables. Sorren gathered himself a small plate of bread and rice and another cup of juice.

Returning to his place by the fire, Sorren found Thale sitting nearby. He was leaning awkwardly to the side, a cup in his good hand, his tovocular eye pointing at the fire, slowly twisting around. The colors of the flames glinted on its lens.

Sorren sat next to him and held out his plate. "Hungry?"

Thale shook his head, grimacing. "Maewyn's medicine took away my appetite." He shifted his arm in his sling. "And my sense of taste."

"A mouthful of bread might bring it back."

Thale only shook his head, keeping his gaze on the fire

before them.

Sorren stuck some bread in his mouth. He didn't have much of an appetite either, but he knew he needed to eat something.

Thale was obviously not happy about having to stay in Owl's Grave. Sorren couldn't blame him, but there was nothing for it. Part of Sorren wanted to explain himself, wanted to remind Thale just how he'd been injured, wanted to remind Thale of the void they'd both seen, that terrible trembling twisting tunnel to a great nothingness in the sky. But what good would it do?

"Have you seen any owls?" Sorren asked. "You have the better eye."

Thale sipped his drink. "Plenty of owls. They stay high in the trees. They keep closer to the sky."

Sorren looked skyward, but all was twisted branches and shadow above. "I've only seen one."

"They know who you are." Thale said it as if he almost wanted to laugh. "That's what Maewyn says. So they must be afraid of you. Do you know why they call this place Owl's Grave?"

"Something to do with death?"

"They come here to die for some reason," Thale said. "They come to Maewyn. She holds them until they die and then she burns them."

"Strange."

Thale gathered some dead twigs and leaves in his hand and tossed them into the fire. The leaves blackened and shriveled and shrunk until their ashes flittered away in the sparks.

Sorren was suddenly filled with visions of his father being sucked through that tunnel into the void, his body writhing and twisting and deforming in the vortex.

How was he supposed to defeat Atlorus? How could he do what his father could not?

Sorren bit off another piece of bread and washed it down with a gulp of juice. "You never told me what Atlorus had in his hand," he said quietly. "What did he use to create that void?"

And now Thale turned to face Sorren, his tovocular eye winding backward. "It was a small black crystal." He set down his cup and held up his hand, imitating the size of the crystal with his fingers. "I could only see a bit of it. He was holding it tightly."

Sorren sipped his drink slowly. How could Atlorus be the chosen one of a prophecy if his power depended on a weapon? He could not have been born with the black crystal in his hand. Someone had given him that tove. Someone here in Owl's Grave.

Where was Maewyn? Sorren glanced around the bonfire. He hadn't seen her since he returned from the hunt.

"We need a new story."

Sorren turned to find a young girl at his side, seven or eight years old. She was cloaked in light brown bear fur with white rabbit skin draped over her shoulders, rabbit paws dangling beside her arm.

"A story?" Sorren repeated, noticing a small group of children watching him from a distance.

"Do you know any stories?" the girl asked, glancing back

and forth between Sorren's mechanical arm and Thale's tovocular eye.

"Oh, forgive me," Rozzom said, appearing behind the girl and putting his hands on her shoulders. "I told them they could ask you if you knew any stories. They've grown bored with our tales. We tell them the same stories over and over. But that was last night. Tonight, we'll leave you alone." He gently began pushing the girl back toward her group of friends.

"I know a story," Sorren said, looking at the girl. "Have you ever heard of the maker of the twenty-first moon?"

The girl shook her head.

Moments later, Sorren had reversed his direction on the log so that his back was to the fire. A small group of seven young children sat before him on the forest floor. In their thick fur clothing, they looked like they were wrapped up in blankets, ready for bed. They watched Sorren intently and seemed to focus mostly on the movements of his silver-copper arm.

Sorren told the short story of the maker of the twenty-first moon as he remembered it, embellishing things here and there as he saw fit. He wasn't sure he was a particularly great storyteller, but he found he held the children's attention well enough. For a few moments, he forgot about Atlorus and the crystal and the void, instead trying to recall the way his father had told him stories in their castle, the way his voice and pacing had made almost every word feel important. Though Sorren could still hear his father's warm fireside voice somewhere inside, it was distant now, like a memory from someone else's life.

As Sorren approached the part of the story in which the

main character beheaded the man he feared was a wizard, he considered that perhaps the story was too dark for some of the younger children. Perhaps he should somehow change the ending so as not to frighten anyone.

They sat before him, staring at him with their wide white eyes.

No, Sorren thought, *they'll hear the real ending. It's part of the story.*

The children were dead-quiet as Sorren raised his walking stick over his head with his mechanical arm, imitating a soldier's sword preparing to strike.

Sorren spoke slowly. "Turning his eyes from the moons in the sky, he took one last glance at the crying man kneeling before him. He told him to hold his head up high, so that his blade would not miss his neck. And then, in the stillness of the forest—"

Quove dove down from somewhere, squawking madly before swiftly fluttering back into the darkness.

Clang!

Something struck Sorren's mechanical forearm from behind, and his walking stick tumbled from the grip of his silver-copper fingers.

Children gasped. Adults let out cries of surprise.

Sorren turned to see what had struck him. It was there, beside the log, nestled among the dead pine needles of the forest floor. It looked like a small brown leather pouch of sand.

Sorren recognized it in a heartbeat.

Devil's breath.

A hand bomb, the same sort of bomb soldiers had thrown

at him in his castle.

As it began to quiver, Sorren leapt to his feet and held out his flesh-and-blood hand. He thought the seizing spell, bringing the bomb hurdling into his palm, and, with another spell, sent it rocketing skyward.

Boom!

The air shook and Sorren felt the heat of the fire above on his cheeks, but his eyes were scanning the darkness between the trees.

"There," Thale said, pointing at an angle through the colors of the bonfire.

Sorren followed Thale's finger, but saw nothing but trees and shadow. More small leather pouches burst through the pine branches, rolling through the air at Sorren. He threw his arms out in their direction, as if placing his hands on an invisible wall, catching the bombs with a spell and launching them into the forest canopy high above.

Boom! Boom! Boom!

Men and women were scrambling around the bonfire, dropping plates, spilling bowls, overturning tables. The children were screaming.

The children.

Sorren spun around. Some of them had already fled into the forest, but others crouched close to the ground, some shielding their eyes, others gazing skyward, transfixed by the sight of the bombs bursting above. Black ash from the explosions came drifting down like fine snow.

Sorren flung his silver-copper hand in their direction, back-handing the air, swiftly but gently pushing the children backward as if by the winds of an invisible storm, backward into the shadows where they'd be safe.

More bombs thudded against the ground beside Sorren's feet. He aimed an arm in their direction as he saw them, whispering spells under his breath, casting the bombs skyward as quickly and forcefully as possible.

Boom! Boom! Boom!

Branches snapped and plunged to the ground as ash continued raining down. Thale grunted.

Sorren turned to see him two steps away, fallen on his side, desperately clambering to pull himself back up, his good hand clawing at the log.

A bomb came soaring out from the shadows, smashing into the weaving colors of the bonfire's flames, sending a spray of sparks showering across Sorren and Thale. Sorren pointed a hand at the fire, trying to spot the bomb within the roaring flames, but it was no use. The flames were too bright and wild.

Sorren turned his flesh-and-blood arm to Thale and whispered a spell, preparing to send Thale blowing back to safety as he'd done with the children. He pointed his mechanical arm at the flames, directing the same spell at the bonfire's wood, hoping to catapult the whole blazing thing skyward in the opposite direction.

Just as Thale began rising into the air, just as the bonfire's colorful flames began whirling back and away, the bomb exploded.

TWENTY-ONE

SOUNDLESS FLASH of light and Sorren flipped backward, fire rushing past his eyes in wild torrents of color. He put his arms over his head, curling himself up as large chunks of burning debris fell upon him, pelting him from head to toe. Fortunately, nothing heavy enough to cause injury, but it hurt all the same, stinging his back, scalding his injured leg and the back of his flesh-and-blood hand.

It was over in seconds, and Sorren was quick to his feet, shaking off ash and surveying what remained, ready to catch more hand bombs with a spell should they come flying toward him.

Nearby, Thale slowly and crookedly rose to his feet.

A long shaft of burning wood impaled his side. Thale had it clutched in his good hand, oblivious to its flames, slowly pulling it out, blood dripping from its end.

"Don't touch it!" Sorren wasn't sure if he said the words or only thought them as he stumbled toward Thale.

But it was too late; Thale dropped the burning length of timber by his feet. In vain, he pressed a hand against the gaping wound in his side, blood pouring out from between his fingers, and he collapsed forward.

Sorren caught him and the two fell to the forest floor.

Sorren sat up with Thale in his arms. He pressed his silver-copper hand on Thale's wound, but the warm blood oozed out all the same, drenching his silver hand and soaking his shirt.

Thale began shuddering, convulsing, his body thrashing backward in violent jerks. His human eye fluttered and his tovocular eye twisted in strange erratic rhythms. His breath became desperate gasps.

"I . . . I should've . . ." Thale's voice came in strained broken whispers. "I should've . . . should've seen them . . ."

Sorren tried to work his flesh-and-blood hand under Thale's head to steady it. The blood wouldn't stop.

Then Thale was still. His human eye relaxed and almost seemed to glow, as if he'd caught sight of something wondrous and beautiful in the sky.

His body went limp. A long breath escaped his mouth and the life in his eye was gone.

Sorren wasn't sure how long he sat there with his friend in his arms. Time had stopped.

The rest of the world was gone. Silent. Dark. Cold.

Sorren drew a deep breath and took his mechanical hand from the wound. Gently, he put three blood-soaked silver fingers around Thale's tovocular eye and pulled it from his socket. Blood dripped across Thale's face as Sorren clasped the gold-blue eye in his silver-copper palm.

When he glanced up, he found several men watching him. Rozzom in his wolf skins, Entackus in his bear skins, another man in tiger skins. They stood amid the burning remnants of the exploded bonfire, their faces expressionless. Behind them, half hidden by the shadows of the forest, more men of Owl's Grave stood beside four kneeling Zolen soldiers. Swords rested against the soldiers' necks as someone tied their hands behind their backs.

Rozzom and Entackus stepped forward and knelt beside Sorren. Rozzom slid a hand across Thale's face, closing his lifeless human eye, then he and Entackus carefully took Thale's body from Sorren's arms. They said nothing as they began carrying the body back toward their huts.

They saw me cast those spells, Sorren thought. *They know who I am now.*

He kept silent as he stood up, and he didn't look back as he walked past the captured Zolen soldiers and into the shadows of the forest.

TWENTY-TWO

THE FOREST was almost pitch black, but Sorren followed the soft and steady sounds of Quove's wings as the raven led him to the airship. He held his arms out in front of him and walked slowly, careful to not walk headfirst into a tree. He wasn't so concerned about the branches, letting them scrape his face as he walked past them.

He had to keep moving. He didn't want to linger in the forest or in the memory of what had just happened. *Keep moving*, he told himself. *Don't stop moving.*

He needed the moon. The sudden thirst for a clear open view of the Nyrish moon was almost unbearable.

Sorren had no idea how long he'd been walking when he came to the airship. It sat on the forest floor, tilting to the side as if about to fall over. The loading bridge was open, casting a faint yellow glow across the surrounding trees.

Sorren approached, realizing he'd been letting himself limp.

"Sorren?" Sage called out, carefully walking down the

crooked slope of the loading bridge. "It's not midnight yet—Sorren?" Now he was hurrying down the bridge. "Sorren, what happened?"

Sorren held out his mechanical arm. "Get me my staff."

"You're bleeding all over!" Sage said, adjusting his spectacles. "You need to lie—"

"My staff," Sorren repeated, almost shouting.

Sage paused and stood there, staring at him with wide worried eyes.

Don't make me say it again, Sorren thought.

As if reading his mind, Sage turned and hurried back into the airship. Moments later, he reemerged with the staff, the green flame at its top blazing brightly. Sorren uttered the seizing spell, sending it rushing out of Sage's grasp, catching it in his silver-copper hand. *Clank.*

Sage rubbed his hands together. "It's not midnight yet. The ship's not ready."

Sorren limped closer to the airship. "Get me a pen and paper."

Sage looked confused, but once again disappeared into the airship, returning moments later with the pen and a scroll. "What's all this about? What happened to you?"

With another spell, Sorren pulled the pen and paper from Sage's grip and caught them in his other hand, stuffing them into a coat pocket. "They know who I am," he said as he turned away. "And Thale is dead."

He heard no response from Sage as he followed his raven back into the forest, this time with the light of his staff to guide his steps.

* * * * *

SORREN JOURNEYED up a long steep hill where half-buried boulders glinted in the green fire of his staff. The pine trees thinned out here, and the ground was hard and rocky. Quove flew ahead, leading Sorren up the hillside.

As he continued climbing, pieces of the Nyrish moon came into view between the trees and boulders ahead. Such small pieces, but the dark warm shades of blue beckoned Sorren forward.

The hill peaked with a smooth surface, a narrow gently-sloping plateau that led to a sharp cliff. Sorren walked to its edge and peered over, kicking pebbles into the pools of darkness below. It was a long way down.

Here above the pines of Owl's Fortress, the wide sky was open and crowded with stars. The full moons cast their light upon the sea of treetops as dark clouds scrolled across the distant horizons.

Sorren sat down and unrolled the blank scroll across the hard ground. He licked the tip of the fountain pen and wrote out a small note to Kovola, informing him of what had happened in Owl's Grave and why he'd never see Thale again. When he finished, he ripped the note from the rest of the paper and rolled it into a small tight scroll. He used the tip of the fountain pen to tear off a very thin strip of cloth from where his coat was still ripped open on his arm. He whistle Quove to his mechanical hand, placed her on his foot, and carefully tied the note to Quove's leg with the cloth.

Before sending the raven on her errand, Sorren sat back and looked at the bird. Why had she come to him in the first place? He'd never questioned it before. He took the bird in his hands, held her close for moment, and quietly spoke her name. "Quove." Slowly, he held her out and gave her to the sky. She flew off, out over the trees of Owl's Fortress. Sorren watched until she was too small to see.

Then Sorren stood and faced to the Nyrish moon. He didn't *need* to collect power, he had plenty coursing through his veins. But he was thirsty for it.

He opened his mind and let the Nyrish power flood in. It flowed through him and around him and seemed to cloak him in warmth. It brought him back to that stormy night in the castle years ago, when he'd drawn a fever and only found comfort beside the fire.

He let the power rush in, knowing he didn't need it, knowing he was already overflowing. It wasn't wise to drink in too much Nyrish power. It might escape in wild and dangerous ways. It might break his mind.

But Sorren wasn't worried. He would drown in the power tonight. He tried to open his mind more, to let more power in. Images burst into existence before his eyes. His castle crumbling to pieces. A ring of ravens flying in circles. The wizards of the Nyrish Council sitting around their table, scowling at him and shaking their heads. The rire, the breeze caressing its fur, steaming blood bursting from its neck. Atlorus sitting in the center of a bonfire, unharmed by the roaring flames around him, staring through them with a fearless smile. The power was rushing in and around Sorren's mind like a raging river, pushing his thoughts into strange and ghastly places, yet Sorren wanted more.

He lost all feeling in his body. He lost all sense of sight and sound, all sense of up and down. He felt weightless now, as if he were floating in some warm abyss where he existed only as a collection of strange and broken thoughts.

And the roaring river of power began ripping at his mind, tearing at its edges, searching for a way to burst through, pulling apart his consciousness. So Sorren laughed, or thought laughter, and let go of his mind, surrendering himself to a deep and dreamless sleep.

SORREN AWOKE to a cold wind. The stars were hidden by clouds, but the Nyrish moon still shone through, coloring the clouds a creamy blue.

Something soared above, its silhouette gliding in circles. Quove? No. The shape wasn't right. This was a larger bird. As it flapped its wings and swooped down, its wide golden eyes glinted in the green light of Sorren's staff.

An owl.

Sorren stretched and sat up, grabbing his staff and pointing it at the owl, letting the flow of his power brighten the staff's green flame. It wasn't just any owl. Sorren was sure he recognized it. It was the owl that had watched him slay the rire.

As Sorren rose to his feet, the owl flew down the rocky hillside to the edge of the forest. Then it came fluttering back toward Sorren, then back to the trees.

It wants me to follow, Sorren realized. He glanced around his feet to be sure nothing had fallen from his pockets, then started forward, following the gray owl into the forest.

Sorren kept his eyes on the owl as he descended the gentle slopes into the thick forest underbrush. The owl flew slowly, always circling back toward Sorren now and then as if to make sure he was still following. Its wide golden eyes were like those of a madman, curious and bewildered and confused by everything he saw.

The winds rushed through the trees, twisting branches, making them writhe like the arms of monsters searching for prey. Sorren kept his eyes on the owl, brushing his hair from his eyes every few minutes. The owl led Sorren deeper and deeper into Owl's Fortress, down countless hills and slopes as the forest grew thicker and the trees grew wider, their roots breaking through the rocky ground and webbing across the forest floor like a mess of giant tangled snakes.

Sorren's legs grew tired, his injured leg causing him to almost stagger along. The icy wind made him shiver, and when he clutched at his coat, he noticed that Thale's blood had dried and darkened across his shirt.

At long last, Sorren found himself standing on an unnaturally rectangular stone pressed into the ground. Just ahead, more stones stretched on, winding down a hillside between two large stone walls. As Sorren realized he'd been led to a staircase of some sort, the owl landed on his shoulder, its long talons gently digging into his skin.

Sorren began descending the staircase. The steps were crooked and uneven, some half-covered in dirt. Weeds and wildflowers grew between cracks in the stone; the staircase had obviously been made long ago, and was losing a slow battle with the ever-changing forest.

Venturing down between the stone walls was almost like venturing into a cave, but there was no roof overhead, only the barely visible swaying branches of the trees, so high above that they seemed like part of the sky. The space between the walls grew narrow and the staircase wound this way and that. The green flame of Sorren's staff sent sharp black shadows stretching across the path ahead.

Sorren smelled incense in the cold air, the same sort of incense he'd smelled in his hut when he'd first wakened from his injuries.

Stepping around one last bend of the staircase, Sorren came to a wide circular stone room without a ceiling. The flat stone floor was covered in strange symbols: a bird, a moon, a candle, a sword, a lion. Many other shapes he didn't recognize. The walls were half-covered in dirt and moss. Words were etched into them, writing in a language Sorren couldn't read. Countless sticks of incense stood in tall vases that lined the walls, coils of smoke twisting into the air, filling the room with a gray haze. Two mighty orange-pink flames roared in what looked like giant pots, casting dancing beams of light through the smoke.

Between the flames, sitting on a throne of stone with an enormous book spread across her lap, was Maewyn.

As Maewyn glanced up from the book, the owl soared across the room, breaking through the haze and landing beside Maewyn on the throne's right arm.

Maewyn turned to the owl and smiled, stroking its feathers. "This is Chronicle, my owl." She glanced back at Sorren. "He's over eight-hundred years old. No ordinary owl. He's seen the cycles of the world." Maewyn gently closed her book and leaned forward, resting her arms on the book's wide cover. "Why did he lead you here, Sorren?"

Sorren stepped forward, trying to get a better look at Maewyn. Perhaps the haze was playing tricks with the light, but the flame of his staff seemed to grow more blue as he neared Maewyn's throne; it became almost teal. "You recognize the staff?" he asked.

"I do," Maewyn said, "but I knew it was you on the night we found you."

"You've seen me before?"

"No. But there are other sources of power besides your Nyrish moon. You are not the only one here with powers, Sorren."

"Did everyone know?"

"I told no one," Maewyn said. "You came to Owl's Fortress for a reason. I have to let your story take its course."

"My story?"

"I have to be careful with what knowledge I share," Maewyn said. "The cycles of the world are delicate. One must be allowed to make his own decisions based on what he knows, even when those decisions lead to tragedy. It's all part of the cycle."

Sorren took another step forward. "Were you there when it happened?"

"When what happened?"

"When Thale . . ." Sorren couldn't finish the sentence. Already the memory seemed like something from a dream.

"When Thale was killed?" Maewyn asked. "No. I've been

here for some time. But I knew something treacherous was coming. Thale's death is part of the reason you came to Owl's Fortress."

"I didn't come to this forest for a purpose," Sorren said. "My airship crashed."

"It may not have been *your* purpose at that moment. We are part of a cycle that works beyond our intents and desires. Everything happens for a reason, and your decisions determine your past as much as your future."

"You burn a lot of incense, don't you?"

Maewyn only smiled. "I sound like a lunatic. I only see too much. In this realm, we experience time like an arrow, the unchangeable past behind us, the unknowable future ahead. But beyond our realm, there is no time. Only a great eternity. Our stories exist all at once," Maewyn tapped the cover of the book on her lap, "like a stack of pages. And they bend and fold as one. That is what makes prophecies possible."

"Prophecies are . . . page folds from the future?"

Maewyn laughed, shaking her head. "Prophecies come from seeing the story as a whole. You are here now. There is a reason for it. There is something you must learn here."

"I only followed your owl."

Maewyn put a hand on the back of the owl. "Chronicle became part of your story. He saw that you needed to be here for some reason. You may not be able to see it yet. Perhaps it is something you will never understand in this realm at all."

Sorren glanced at the symbols under his feet. A coiled snake, a chalice, a rosebush.

He remembered he wanted to ask Maewyn something. He

looked up. "Atlorus killed my father with a small black crystal that opens a portal to an abyss," he said. "Did you give it to him?"

"Ah," Maewyn said, "I did not realize you knew about the weapon."

"Someone must've given it to him. Where did it come from?"

"A good question," Maewyn said. "But I cannot give you a complete answer. I can only tell you that his mother gave him the crystal. It had been part of her family for generations. She knew she would give birth to the Chosen One. Using the crystal to open the portal takes a sort of power itself."

"But he still needs the crystal . . ." Sorren thought aloud. "Is it possible that if someone else in his family, generations earlier or later, had been given the crystal, that *someone else* could've used it to fulfill the Candlewood Prophecy?"

Maewyn turned her eyes skyward, seemingly confused. "That is something I do not know. I cannot see. Too many things have to come to pass." She shook her head and looked at Sorren. "But it doesn't matter. Atlorus *is* the Chosen One now. And *you* are part of the prophecy too. I can see that you understand this all too well."

Sorren leaned on his staff. He wanted to ask Maewyn for everything she knew about the Candlewood Prophecy. But the question that came first slipped out without thinking. "Is Atlorus going to kill me? Is the prophecy unchangeable?"

"By their nature, prophecies are unchangeable," Maewyn said. "They have already been fulfilled, in a sense. Page folds from the future, as you understood it. But the Candlewood

Prophecy—"

Chronicle turned his mad-eyed head and shrieked, flailing his gray and black wings.

Maewyn shushed the bird, petting the feathers on his back, calming him down. "Yes, yes. I know, Chronicle. I must be careful what I say." She turned back to Sorren. "I do not have all the answers myself, after all, so it would be foolish, if not dangerous, for me to speculate. But as you may guess, there is more to the prophecy than has been revealed in any book. Consider what you hold in your hand."

Sorren gazed at his staff, letting its teal flame blind his eyes for a moment. What did the staff have to do with the prophecy?

Maewyn leaned forward. "A miracle it survived, isn't it?"

Sorren had never thought about it. His imagination had been consumed with images of his father's body twisting into the void. He had never considered the staff. How *had* it survived? And hadn't Atlorus insisted on facing his father alone? Why?

"But it's not the prophecy you fear, is it?" Maewyn said, leaning back in her throne with her eyes closed. "I see what you fear now. It's not the threat of death." She opened her eyes. "You're afraid of who you are. You're afraid if you find out who you are, you won't like it. And so you do not look."

Sorren wasn't sure what to say. He almost wanted to laugh. "I am Sorren, son of a dark wizard, heir to the throne of Morrowgrand."

"You know *what* you are," Maewyn said. "But you're afraid of *who* you are. And so you look outside yourself. Your name, your age, your relations. Your looks, your accomplishments. Your desires. Your power. But you know you search in vain."

"So who am I?"

"No one can tell you. But you will not look if you're afraid. And you will not find if you will not look. And for that you are a fool."

"I seem to hear that a lot."

"Yet you don't listen," Maewyn said. "I can give you this warning: If watching Thale die in your arms was difficult for you, then you are not prepared for the path you are taking."

"That's rather vague. You could just as well tell me to beware."

"The path you are taking will affect countless lives," Maewyn said. "You must travel it with caution."

"If you think I'm on the wrong path, why don't you stop me?"

"We both know I cannot," Maewyn said.

"But you *do* think I'm on the wrong path?" Sorren asked.

Maewyn nodded. "You are a fool who makes foolish choices."

"Whose side are you on?"

"Side?"

"Atlorus wants to kill me and take my kingdom. I'm working to stop him. You knew him, you watched him grow up. You only just met me, and you know I'm a dark wizard. Which one of us do you want to succeed?"

Again, Maewyn laughed and shook her head. "The question makes no sense to me. It's like asking who I want to be born a hundred years ago. There is only one way your conflict will end, and I've already seen it."

"Then why are you warning me? If the end can already be seen, why do my choices matter?"

"Because *you* are creating that end. Don't you understand? Just because I can see the end doesn't make your decisions any less yours. You know how yesterday ended, do you not? Yet that does not mean the choices you made then didn't matter."

Sorren didn't bother trying to understand. "I'm only wondering if I can trust you in regards to what I'm doing. Or if your preferred path for me would lead me to my grave."

"An understandable concern," Maewyn said, "but one I can offer no help with. I can only warn you that your current path is dangerous and foolish."

"I hope Chronicle didn't lead me here for only the sake of an obscure warning."

Maewyn shrugged. "Owls are full of wisdom and madness. It's hard to tell the difference sometimes."

Sorren made no response. He twisted the staff in his silver-copper hand, watching shadows from the blue-green light flicker across the gray owl's face. The old creature didn't seem to care. The bird just sat there, staring back at Sorren with his wide wild eyes.

Well, what is it? Sorren thought. *Why did you bring me here?*

When no answer came, Sorren turned to go. "Will you see to it that Thale is buried somewhere the sun can find?"

"They're burying him now," Maewyn said.

As she said it, the low tones of a long bone whistle echoed through the air, barely audible, but definitely there. Sorren recognized the sound and the melody it played. "Atovin's lullaby."

"Every night," Maewyn nodded. "The lyrics are right over here." She pointed to a stretch of foreign words chiseled into the round wall on the side.

Sorren walked over to the words, brushing his flesh-and-blood fingers over the grooves that formed the letters, digging out some of the moss and dirt that had worked its way inside. "It looks like old Tavendin," he said. "I can't read it."

"I know," Maewyn said. "You would've recognized it. It's the Candlewood Prophecy."

Sorren glanced back at Maewyn. "Atlorus's mother plays a lullaby based on the Candlewood Prophecy every night?"

Maewyn nodded. "Part of the prophecy, anyway. Strange that she would play it while they bury Thale. Perhaps she can sense the connection."

Sorren imagined Thale's body in a shallow grave, the wet dirt swallowing him, Atovin's shadow stretching over the grave as she played a lullaby meant for someone else.

Sorren realized he'd been staring at Chronicle, and something clicked in his mind.

Atovin.

The bone whistle.

The lullaby.

In that moment, Sorren understood how to defeat Atlorus.

He turned to Maewyn and smiled. "Goodbye, Maewyn. I found what I came for."

Without waiting for a reply, he turned to the winding stone staircase and left. Chronicle began shrieking again.

TWENTY-THREE

"SAGE!" Sorren called out, striding up the airship's loading bridge. "Sage!"

Sage appeared in the doorway to the cargo room, his face blank, as though he'd been pondering death for the past few hours.

"Sage, I need you to do me a favor."

Sage said nothing.

"You may not like it."

Silence.

Sorren approached Sage and lowered his voice. "We're close to the end now. I know how to defeat Atlorus. But I need your help, and you may not be comfortable with what I need you to do."

Sage stared back at him. Sorren could tell he had questions on his mind, but no heart to ask them. Questions about Thale, questions about what this whole battle was worth. Sorren would not have answered them anyway.

"Will you help me?" Sorren asked. "Or do you wish to stay in Owl's Grave?"

"What do you need?" Sage asked, his voice a whisper.

S AGE DID AS Sorren asked and the two spoke nothing of it. They kept the door to the airship's cargo room locked as they began their journey away from Owl's Fortress. Along with his favor for Sorren, Sage had brought some food and drink from Owl's Grave to keep their stomachs full. Whether Sage had asked for it politely or had stolen it, Sorren didn't know and didn't ask. Though he was almost overflowing with Nyrish power, Sorren only let a small stream flow to the airship's engine. He was in no rush to get back to the caverns. Kovola would be waiting, and Sorren wanted Quove to deliver her message before his own arrival.

For the next four days, Sorren and Sage flew the airship across the kingdom in almost complete silence. They took turns at the controls and making sure everything was well in the cargo room.

Sorren spent his free moments polishing his mechanical arm, reflecting on his conversation with Maewyn, and watching the kingdom pass below his window. This was the longest amount of time he'd ever spent away from his castle. He didn't recognize the lands of the kingdom he'd been promised, not from the views of the low valleys they were flying over.

Every now and then, Sorren polished Thale's blue and gold tovocular eye, twisting it in and out between his fingers. The distinct whirring sound it made as the lens turned from side to side always brought Thale's face to mind. Every time Sorren put the eye back in his coat pocket, he promised himself he'd stop fiddling with it. Every few hours, he broke his promise.

On the fourth night, the airship finally arrived in the small stony hills where Sorren's secret caverns were hidden. Sorren offered Sage a room in the caverns, but Sage insisted on staying on the airship, as if the caverns were dangerous or tainted with evil. It didn't matter. They'd only be spending one night there. The next day, they'd be off to the castle, where Sorren planned to face Atlorus once more, or wait for his return. Sorren had considered using a mirror to portal himself back to the castle. But even if Atlorus and his Zolen soldiers had not smashed all the castle's mirrors, as was likely, Sorren did not intend his return to his own castle to be so modest. He'd enter through the front door.

The caverns were as silent as a graveyard as Sorren made his way to his room. He had missed the smell of the place. A dank and dirty smell, but it had started to feel like home. Kovola was most likely asleep somewhere. If so, Sorren didn't want to wake him. Not yet.

As he carefully pushed open the door to his room, Quove came darting from the shadows and perched herself on his shoulders. The note that had been tied to her leg was gone.

In his room, Sorren lit some candles using matches. He sat on his narrow bed and carefully unwrapped the bandages around his leg, discovering that his skin was intact and healthy. Not even the discoloration of a bruise. It now felt as if it had never been injured in the first place.

Sorren examined the area that had stung so much as he'd

walked around Owl's Grave. Had it healed that fast, or had he ever really been injured in the first place? He poked at and rubbed the leg. Not even a hint of soreness.

A shadow crept across the stony cavern floor. Sorren looked up to find Kovola approaching, long strands of unkempt scraggly green hair dangling down in front of his eyes. He walked as if trapped in a deep slumber, every step an automatic thoughtless shuffle forward. His long iron staff clacked beside his feet with every other step.

The old man stopped before Sorren and met his gaze.

"I've realized something," Kovola said, "over these past two days. That I'm as great a fool as you are, for wasting time on you. For wasting any energy worrying about you." The old man's eyes, what Sorren could see of them behind his strands of green hair, were red, and they glistened in the candlelight. "I've already packed my things. My oath to your family be damned." He turned toward the door. "I'm leaving."

Sorren opened his mouth, but no words came.

An oath bound by the Nyrish power could not be broken. By abandoning his oath, Kovola was, in essence, killing himself. He'd be dead before the next sunrise if he broke his oath.

"Kovola," Sorren said, standing up.

Kovola paused at the threshold of the door, but did not turn around.

"Kovola, I order you to leave, and serve my family no more." It was all he could do to save his life.

Kovola made no response. He stood in silence for a moment, then continued out the door.

Sorren changed his clothes, dressing in new pants and a

new coat. He decided to leave on his shirt, now stiff with the dark dried blood of his only friend. He wanted Atlorus to see it.

Sorren sat back down on his bed. There'd be no sleeping tonight. All he had left to do was wait. The key to defeating Atlorus was locked in the airship's cargo room.

TWENTY-FOUR

I N THE CASTLE'S throne room, Atlorus watched the relentless rains stream down the room's grand high windows. Dawn had come hours ago, but the sky was still dark, this part of the kingdom lost in the shadow of a wild and wicked storm.

Atlorus was dressed in the finest clothes he'd ever worn. A dark gray woolen surcoat embroidered with flowing gold patterns, a black silk cloak, and fine brown leather boots, all prepared for him by tailors and seamstresses in the nearby city of Faircliff. His hair had been finely groomed and combed back, ready for the crown.

He was seated on the throne, the only seat in the room. It sat in the center of a broad stone dais, covered with a dark blue rug. The throne itself was uncushioned, tall, and wide, clearly made for a larger man. Still, Atlorus sat up straight, refusing the temptation to lean to any one side.

Gashdane stood on his left, dressed in his usual armor,

which had been polished thoroughly.

A priest, whose name Atlorus had already forgotten, stood on his right, dressed in long robes of red and white.

A small crowd was gathering into the room, attendants directing them to one side or another. They'd have to stand for the short ceremony. Most were not dressed particularly well. Many wore worn-out jackets and faded tattered dresses, but Atlorus didn't care. He'd insisted the coronation be performed swiftly, and he wanted as many witnesses as possible. The small audience had not had much time to prepare.

Gazing down the long aisle that stretched from the dais to the wide iron doors on the opposite side of the room, images of Vonlock seemed to dance before him. It was the way Vonlock had fallen into the void that haunted Atlorus's memories. The dark wizard had not resisted his fate. He'd hurled his staff aside and remained still as Atlorus approached and opened the void. Atlorus had expected Vonlock to attack, to cast some sort of counter-spell, to defend himself with winds or flames from the Nyrish power. But he'd only watched Atlorus with an awful sadness in his eyes and let the void pull him in. It was like he had expected to die that day, and knew it was pointless to resist. More than that, he had seemed sorry, as if he'd been half-hoping Atlorus would change his mind and not fulfill the prophecy after all . . .

But what did it matter now? Vonlock was wicked, his end was justified. Atlorus would be a good king, the sort of king Morrowgrand truly deserved, the king whose coming the prophets had foretold.

"Let's begin," Atlorus said.

"Soon," Gashdane said.

Atlorus turned to him. "Now. We've waited long enough."

"You should put that away," Gashdane said.

At first, Atlorus wasn't sure what he meant. Then he realized he had the black crystal clutched tightly in his palm, his knuckles white. He relaxed his grip, but made no move to pocket the weapon. "I need to keep it close."

"You don't need it," Gashdane said. "You should hide it. It's more important than your crown."

"I could need it at any moment," Atlorus said. "I know how to control it. It's safe with me."

"Very well." Gashdane stepped forward to the edge of dais and cupped a hand next to his mouth. "Close the doors."

Attendants slowly shut the heavy iron doors. The murmurs and whispers of the small crowd faded. There was supposed to be music, fanfares blasting from horns and trumpets, but Atlorus had refused the ritual in order to hurry the ceremony. The only sound was the heavy rain lashing at the windows and the grumbling of distant thunder.

A servant slowly walked down the aisle, holding a thin silver crown on a dark blue velvet pillow. He walked as if on the edge of a cliff, every step precious and cautious.

Atlorus tried to remain absolutely still, counting the passing seconds with his breath. In a few moments, he'd be the king, just as the men and women of Owl's Grave had always promised. For so long, this destiny had seemed too good to be true. But now he was here, just as they'd said.

The crown bearer climbed the steps of the dais and held the crown out to the priest.

The priest took the crown in his wrinkled narrow fingers, uttering prayers in Old Tavendin, his deep gravelly voice echoing through the room with power sufficient to battle the sounds of the storm ranging outside. Lightning flashed across the windows, glinting off the edges of the crown like dancing sparks. The priest held the crown over Atlorus's head and Atlorus closed his eyes, ready to bear the crown's weight and authority.

The priest switched to the common tongue. "On this, the nineteenth day of the third month, I hereby crown—"

Crash!

Atlorus's eyes popped open. The small crowd gasped, their eyes fixed skyward. Gashdane drew his sword.

Atlorus noticed the broken window on the right, storm winds howling through the now empty frame. The icy wind blew across his skin and whipped his hair this way and that.

The crowd pointed at the throne as a large black raven landed on its right side. It stared up at Atlorus and screeched.

"A raven?" Gashdane said.

Something thin and white was tied to its leg. Atlorus carefully undid the string and something fell from the bird's leg, clacking and rolling against the uncushioned throne.

Atlorus recognized it as he picked it up.

A long mammoth bone whistle.

His mother's whistle.

His eyes returned to the raven as he tightened his grip on the black crystal. "Sorren is here."

TWENTY-FIVE

THE IRON DOORS burst open. A blast of air struck Atlorus, flinging him backward, and he struck his head
against the back of the throne. The priest on his right
fell backward, dropping the silver crown at the foot of the
throne. Atlorus leaned forward and reached for it, tossing the
bone whistle down the steps of the dais.

Before he could grab the crown, walls of blue-green flames
erupted along the edges of the room's center aisle, creating a
narrow corridor of fire. In the center of it, at the far end of the
room, was Sorren. His rain-soaked hair clung to his face in
tangled webs. He wore green goggles over his eyes, and the
back of his long black coat thrashed about behind him like a
cloak. He held his father's staff in a silver-copper mechanical
hand, its flame burning green.

Atlorus stood and brought the black crystal to his fore-
fingers. This was a terrible place to open the void, with so
many innocent bystanders crowded close by. Many of them

would no doubt perish.

But there was nothing Atlorus could do about that.

He raised the black crystal, preparing to open the void just above Sorren's head.

But Sorren stepped forward and revealed he was not alone.

Behind him, dressed in dripping-wet animal fur, tied up in ropes and chains, blindfolded and gagged, was Atovin.

"Mother," Atlorus said.

Sorren slid his goggles from his eyes and continued forward. "Where is your void, Atlorus?"

Atlorus swallowed, dropping his arm.

"Atlorus," Gashdane said, his sword pointed at Sorren, "Atlorus, you must do it."

"Are you not the Chosen One?" Sorren said, pulling Atovin stumbling along behind him. "Are you not the one who killed my father?"

"Atlorus, open the void!" Gashdane said.

"But . . ." Atlorus could hardly speak. His mouth was dry. His legs trembled beneath him.

"It's your final test, Atlorus," Gashdane said. "You knew it might come to this."

"Oh, Atlorus," Sorren said. "Where has your power gone?" It looked as if the dark wizard's shirt was stained with blood.

"Now!" Gashdane said. "Now! Before he gets closer!"

Sorren pointed his staff at Gashdane, who was instantly hurled backward, flipping through the air like a ragdoll. He crashed against a side wall and his body crumpled against the stone floor, leaving him groaning in pain.

Sorren took one more step forward, then paused. "The

choice is yours, Atlorus," he said. "You who have taken everything from me, I offer myself to you. Are you not willing to lose what you are willing to take?"

Atlorus sat back down on the throne, his arms shaking.

Sorren just stood there, watching, waiting.

Atlorus took deep breaths. His mother's lullaby seemed to fill the air, as if part of his mind had escaped to a dream.

This was not part of the prophecy. He'd never been warned his own mother would have to die by his own hand.

Slowly, he raised the black crystal once more. He aimed the spell to open the void just below Sorren's feet. Just a thought and it would be over. Just one little thought to open the void.

But he'd have to watch his mother fall into that black abyss.

There had to be another way. If the prophecy was true, there had to be another way. This was not the time.

He lowered the black crystal.

Sorren stepped forward, climbing up the dais, leaving Atovin on the aisle. Now he was so close that opening the void was impossible, unless Atlorus was willing to sacrifice himself.

Could he? Was he willing to die for this? Perhaps his own life was the true price of fulfilling the prophecy.

He slowly raised his arm one last time, but Sorren caught it in his icy human hand. He leaned his staff against the throne and forced Atlorus's fingers open with his mechanical hand, his silver fingers cold and hard as iron.

Atlorus thought the spell to create the void under the throne, but it was too late. Sorren took the black crystal in his silver-copper hand. He held it up and examined it as lightning burst through the windows and thunder shook the air.

"I will not call you weak," Sorren said. "We were both made to bear such darkness." He clutched the crystal in his hand, took his staff, and met Atlorus's eyes. "But you were not born to be a king. And I am stronger." He knelt down, curling his fingers around the silver crown. "You can keep the castle," he said, "but I'm taking the crown. I have another throne."

Atlorus felt the blood drain from his face. He could hardly move. Could this really be happening?

He'd lost. He'd failed the kingdom. He'd failed the world.

The flames that had trapped the small crowds on each side of the aisle faded away. The men and women stared up at Sorren, frozen in fear. Children were crying, but no one made efforts to comfort them.

"People of Morrowgrand," Sorren announced, stepping down the dais, "put no hope in your savior. Atlorus will not be your king. His prophecies will not come true." Sorren passed Atovin, leaving her standing there tied up and blindfolded. He made his way down the aisle, toward the open iron doors. "I will return soon, and I will make a new kingdom from the shadows of what my father left behind. Continue with your songs and celebrations if you wish. Curse my name and spit on my father's grave. I do not need your prayers for the world I am building." He paused at the door's threshold, turning back to the small crowd in the room as his raven flew to his shoulder. "But for your own sake, remember this day and remember my face. Prepare for what is coming. I will return soon."

Then Sorren turned and vanished into the shadows beyond the door.

For ten heartbeats, there was silence, nothing but the tortured song of the storm outside. As people began to move and murmur in cautious whispers, Atlorus ran to his mother. He pulled off her gag and blindfold and the ropes and chains that bound her. Then they stood there clinging to each other, trapped in each other's embrace, and spoke nothing.

TWENTY-SIX

ORREN STOOD on the top deck of his royal airship, the same place Atlorus had stood when he'd created the portal to the void over Owl's Fortress.

The airship had been easy to commandeer. The few Zolen soldiers that had been guarding it had not put up much of a fight after Sorren demonstrated that he could fling their bodies from his path with little more than a thought. Some soldiers had called out for Atlorus, but of course their cries were left unanswered.

Sage was flying the ship, a task he seemed to enjoy, especially after Sorren promised he could keep it in exchange for flying him around for the next year or so. When Sage asked what had happened with Atovin, whom he had kidnapped for him, Sorren replied, "Family reunion."

They were flying out over the cold eastern seas to the Atrolius Kingdom, where the Nyrish Council met in a tower in the mountains by the coast. Most wizards would use mirror portals to get there from across their scattered castles around the world, but the tower was close enough to Morrowgrand's borders that an airship could fly there in only four or five hours.

Sorren leaned over the rail, rolling the black crystal from hand to hand. It was only this small weapon that had made Atlorus anything, only this small weapon that had torn Sorren's life apart.

Sorren still carried Thale's small tovocular eye in his pocket. He knew he'd have to return to Owl's Fortress someday to see Thale's grave. For now, the eye would be a reminder of that.

He also wanted to ask Maewyn more questions. Surely the woman kept many more secrets than Sorren could know.

Watching the blue light of the Nyrish moon gleam along the edges of the black crystal, Sorren wondered if his Nyrish power could be used to activate the weapon and open a portal to the void. Somewhere, deep in the back of his mind, like a bizarre memory from a half-remembered dream, Sorren knew he could. If he tried it and practiced it a bit, he knew he could use the weapon just as Atlorus had.

Which meant, at this moment, with the black crystal in his hand, Sorren was the most powerful being in the world, completely unstoppable.

He raised the black crystal in his flesh-and-blood hand, pointing it at the stars.

Then he flung the weapon out into the sea.

It fell into the black waters below and was gone.

No one would ever be able to open a portal to the void again.

Sorren took a deep breath, closed his eyes, and enjoyed the chill of the frigid salty sea wind on his face.

TWENTY-SEVEN

"WE SHOULD'VE disbanded," Mordock said.

Oakren scoffed, taking a long sip from his chalice. "At least the Chosen One is defeated. He won't be a threat to anyone else now."

"I suppose," Mordock said, "but I'd rather Sorren had been destroyed."

The eight wizards of the Nyrish Council sat around their long black marble table. The clocks were chiming midnight as they waited for their new Head of Council to arrive and take his seat.

"What's so terrible about Sorren, anyway?" the young wizard at the end of the table asked.

"He doesn't listen," Mordock said. "He has no respect."

"The real trouble," an old wizard said, "is that he's powerful. More powerful than any of us."

"The worst thing about him," Oakren said, "is that he always gets what he wants."

Just then, the door at the other end of the room groaned open and Sorren stepped through, his green-fire staff in his silver-copper hand and his black raven on his shoulder.

The torches that lined the walls dimmed, and the air grew cold.

The other wizards were silent as the new Head of Council walked around the table, most of them avoiding eye contact. He stood in front of his empty chair at the end of the table, put his staff against the chair, and filled his chalice from a nearby pitcher. Taking a small sip, he smacked his lips.

"Do I make you so glum?" Sorren asked. "I am not my father."

"We know," Oakren said.

"You must understand," Mordock said, "most of us are more than five times your age. Your lack of experience may be . . . a problem."

"And yet," Sorren said, setting down his chalice, "you had no problem designing a trial meant to kill me?"

"Well," Mordock shifted in his seat. "That was . . . uh . . ."

"Naive," Sorren said, "because you doubted me. You'll learn not to do that." He sat in his chair and leaned forward, folding his hands together around the chalice in front of him. Quove hopped down from his shoulder and stood by his hands. Sorren took another small sip from his cup. "This council has so much more power than you men seem to realize."

"Sorren," Oakren said, "we *do* operate with limits. It can be very dangerous to—"

"Do you realize the sorts of things we can do with the world?" Sorren said, smiling.

"We can't be careless," an old wizard said. "There is a fine balance to—"

"I have magnificent plans for us," Sorren said. "For the world. Best prepare, old men. I'm changing everything. We're starting something new."

End of Book One

LEAVE A REVIEW?

As an indie-published book, reviews have a *tremendous* effect on a book's success. If you enjoyed SON OF A DARK WIZARD, please consider supporting the book by leaving a review for it on Goodreads or your favorite book-selling website.
Thank you!

MY NEWSLETTER

Want to stay updated on my latest releases and offers?
Sign up for my email newsletter at:
morrowgrand.com/thescroll

MY ALBUMS

If you enjoyed my book, you might also enjoy my music!
I compose orchestral music inspired by film scores, classical music, and of course wizards and dragons.
Check out my albums on my bandcamp page at:
seanpatrickhannifin.bandcamp.com

Enter the discount code **darkwizard**
for an extra 25% off any purchase!

ABOUT THE AUTHOR

Sean Patrick Hannifin's stories have appeared in
Daily Science Fiction and *Buzzy Mag*. He blogs about writing
at www.catchingadragon.com.

He lives in Fredericksburg, Virginia.